"Ok ma, yes, I already know that and yes, I have taken care of it already for the 5th time. Mama, please stop calling me every day about this wedding. It is *my* wedding and y'all not gonna drive me crazy with all this little stuff that I have already taken care of. I know you're excited and just want to help, but I'm cool. I love you and I will talk to you later. Bye!" I said to my mother, as I closed the flip on my Sprint vision phone for the 4th time today of talking to her. I love my mother, but she will drive a person to drink hard liquor before the sun comes up with all her questions and suggestions about this freaking wedding.

I know she is only acting so frantic because she is extremely excited about the fact that I am *finally* getting married after all this time Benji and I have been dealing with each other. However, all this pressure and checking up on me every day, is just too much for me to take.  To be real, she doesn't really even like Benji. But she somehow overlooks all the negative things about him every time she needs a little help with her mortgage or with one of her vehicle payments or maybe even a quick trip to the islands; then he becomes her best friend and she sees no wrong with him.  Once he does something for her, she then tells me that I'd better do whatever it takes to hold on to that good man of mine. "WHATEVER!!!"  All I have to say to that is, money is a powerful tool and whoever was the first to say "more money more problems", they never lied.

My name is Ayana Dubois, actress extraordinaire, well not yet, but one day I will be. That is if my fiancé, Benji would just open his eyes and realize my talent and stop throwing monkey wrenches in my program.

I am what they call a mutt, meaning I have a little of this and that all up in my gene pool.  My mama is a Black Indian with a white daddy; her skin is as dark as coal. My pops is a Louisiana Creole with that good black people wavy hair; he's so light he could pass for white. But, he left us when I was three, so I haven't seen his light bright ass since then, so he's a non-factor.

I am definitely a mixture of them both, with a mocha toffee brown complexion, his wavy black hair, big ole butt and full-lips. I have my mama's high cheekbones, slanted eyes, wide hips, big legs, small waist and height. I am 5'5 ft. tall and I have been told that I am shaped like an hourglass. POW! Most folks say I have somewhat of an exotic look, like some of those video girls. You know, I'm like the ones who although I look black, you can definitely tell by my features that I am not straight out the African bush. Overall, I am an educated, sexy woman who is holding it down for a girl in her early 30's; my Oil of Olay is doing the damn thing!

I like to be modest about my looks, because I realize they aren't going to be here forever. I actually used to be very shy and insecure about how I looked. As a child I looked different from the other black kids and you know how children can be so mean. I believe I gained some confidence when I attended an all-black university, North Carolina A&T State University, and those boys saw me as something very interesting and kind of hot! But now I realize that college boys were all just horney as hell!

Nevertheless, these days, I am preparing to be a happily married woman and my wedding is exactly 2 weeks away. My man and I have already spent at least $150 thousand dollars into this wedding and we still haven't paid for the catering, the reception hall or the entertainment. I mean we have the money to pay for it, but I guess I just didn't anticipate it costing so much. Don't get me wrong, I surely don't want to penny pinch; I have to have the best of the best for every aspect of this wedding.  This is the wedding I have always dreamed of. I used to fantasize of how it would be back in Minneapolis when I was just a little shy brown-skinned, bucked tooth girl with long ponytails and butterfly barrettes. So it just has to be perfect, I've come too far for it to be anything less.

Although I am not a movie star, yet and my wedding probably won't be featured on TLC, I still want to make sure my wedding makes headlines for just being one of the most amazing weddings Charlotte, North Carolina has ever seen; after all I feel I deserve it.  Fourteen years plus off and on in this crazy relationship with Benji and dealing with being a part of "The Game"; I have put in my time and this wedding just has to be spectacular.

Benjimin Sykes, that's my fiancé, my man, my love of the past fourteen years of my life.  Even after all these years that we've been together, well off and on, I still get butterflies and somewhat excited when he walks into a room and I haven't seen him all day. That's how I know the love is deep and real.

So, let me tell you what makes my man so great. Well first of all, my baby definitely has his own unique style and such striking features that he will always catch attention wherever he goes. He has a low cut, a Caesar, a perfectly trimmed goatee and a very athletic build; he used to be a track star in high school. He actually was such a great sprinter that several colleges around the country awarded him with track scholarships. He was supposed to go to North Carolina State University, but the streets and fast money kept him on lock in Greensboro, so he never quite made it to college.

He has a slim, runner's physique, with muscular thighs and calves. Lately, he has been working out in our home gym like a mad man, so he is getting every ripple in his abs and his arms cut up and defined too.  It all just makes the total package on his beautiful 6'0ft honey brown body. When he looks at me with those light brown slanted eyes and smiles at me with those thick full luscious lips; it feels like the first day we met all over again.

We have been through it all, the good, the bad and most definitely the ugly.  He finally proposed last year when he thought that I was gonna leave his ass for real that time. Truth is, I don't know if I was really going to leave and I guess it doesn't matter now. But evidently, I made it seem real enough to him that he decided to straighten himself up. Let me tell you what happened that lead up to this point.

**CHAPTER TWO**

It was the day after I found him messing around with this 18-year old girl, Sparkle, which was her stripper name. She was a dancer at Club Champagne's.

I walked up on them out in his truck in the parking lot of the club. I probably wouldn't have even paid the truck any attention if it wasn't rocking back and forth so hard. As I approached closer to the truck, I could hear a female making sex noises. You know, the "oohs" and "Oh my God's" and heavy breathing and shit. I also heard his voice asking her questions like, "Who's your daddy?" and "Say my name?" and other corny shit like that. He never said that stupid stuff to me because I would have laughed at him. But I guess that's what those young chicken heads liked to hear. Anyways, I ran back to my car and opened up my trunk and pulled out my Louisville Slugger and ran back over to the back of his truck. I paced myself and I swung real steady and hard into his back tinted window. I closed my eyes and once I made contact, the window was shattered to pieces. Once I broke out the back window with the bat and snatched him and that little trick out the truck, I was about to aim for her face but she was real quick to yell out "I'm pregnant!" right before the bat was going to meet with her big nose.

Ok so although that was a stunner... for that moment, that wasn't the first time Benji got some chick pregnant; matter a fact it was actually the 4th time! As far as I know Sparkle was his 4th baby mama with his 5th child.

Let me explain, he had twins with this girl named Shawnice about 8 years ago. I know, I know, you may be saying... but you two have been together for 14 years. So if you do the math...yes we were together 8 years ago. So what kind of fool am I to deal with a dude that did that to me? Well, to be honest, I can't quite answer that at the moment with a good response. Best answer I have is because I loved him and I basically forgave him and agreed to accept the children. But as far as the other 2 children, they occurred during the time when we were broken up; at least that's what he tells me.  We used to break up so much and get right back together, it's hard to know if we were in or out when he knocked those chicks up, so basically I just dealt with it.

However, this Sparkle situation, no mistake or confusion... we *were* together, very together, living together and supposedly trying to work on really getting our lives straight.  So when she told me that she was pregnant that night, I was so disgusted and hurt by the whole ordeal; I knew that was my last straw.  I mean in my mind I was thinking how much could I really take from this man?  Am I just going to stick with him until he creates a fucking football team of babies with every chicken in town?

Okay, so getting back to that night in the Club Champagne parking lot. Once Sparkle told me about her being pregnant, I just looked at him and he didn't debate anything she said.  She was standing there looking stupid, with her glittery one piece stripper costume half on, one 8-inch plastic stripper shoe on and her lace front wig cocked to the side after telling me all this. I looked back at him and he basically just stood there next to the truck, panting and looking like a jackass with nothing on but his wet, bunched up in the front boxers on. He wouldn't even look at me, he just stared down at the pavement and so I knew that she was telling the truth. I just looked at the top of his head with such a look of disappointment and probably insanity, because I still had the bat in my hand. But, an angel must have told me to drop the bat on the ground, so

I did. I just shook my head and walked back to my car.

Once I got in my car, I started bawling hysterically over the fact of what I just witnessed while I was trying to put it all together in my mind. I just stepped on the gas and I began driving so fast that I don't even remember stopping at any lights or even how I got home; it was like my car was on auto pilot and driving itself. I didn't even notice that Benji was following behind me in his truck until I pulled up in front of our two car garage and he almost crashed into the back of my car. I looked in the rear view mirror at him jumping out of his truck, heading for my car and at that very moment I made up in my mind that I was leaving him for good.

I stormed into the house and ran upstairs. He was running behind me on the steps and pulling on my arm trying to talk to me and telling me to just listen to him and that it wasn't what it looked like. I just ignored him and the more he talked and tried to make me seem like I was some kind of idiot and that I didn't actually see what I thought I saw back at the club, the more upset I became. His voice kept going in and out like the teacher on Charlie Brown, "whonk, whonk, whonk". I finally turned towards him in a rage and I began tearing the house up and cussing and screaming at the top of my lungs in a fury about him and that nasty ass stripper.

I had walked into our bedroom and got my large Louis Vuitton duffel out of my closet and frantically began to pull my clothes off the hangers and began throwing them in the bag. I was going back and forth to the dressers pulling out all kinds of stuff, panties, bras, socks, t-shirts and throwing it all in the bag. I wasn't even sure if some of the stuff was mine or his. The whole time he kept taking everything that I put into the bag right back out while he was still telling me to calm down and how sorry he was.

I was getting so frustrated that he had the audacity to try and stop me from being the intelligent woman that I am. He was supposed to just let me leave him because he should have known how bad he disrespected me. He should have known that I was worth way more than what he was treating me like; Right?  Well, he obviously didn't think the same way that I was thinking so I started throwing all his cologne bottles against the wall, breaking the lamps on the floor and tearing paintings off the wall. I was just destroying whatever else was in my path to try and make him leave me alone and let me pack in peace.

At that point he grabbed me by both arms facing him and threw me on the bed, pinned me down with his legs and started kissing me on my neck. He kept telling me how much he loved me and that I couldn't leave him. How much he needed me and that he was so sorry. I was struggling and crying for him to get off me, but he wasn't budging.

He began explaining that he was high ( no different than any other night, mind you!) and that Sparkle was going to have him set up because she knew information about his next big deal. He kept explaining that he had to give her some attention to keep her quiet (translation: sex her like an animal in the back of his truck), so that she would back off him and let him make his money. He said that he had been telling her all along that he had a woman, that he didn't want her and what they had going on was strictly business. So supposedly she was mad that he rejected her and then she began threatening to set him up. Question: Does that sound like bullshit to you too? ; Because I didn't believe not one word of it.

He also added that he would have never gotten that pill popping bitch pregnant. He said she was just a hoe that he did some drug business with in the strip club. He did admit that he was only with her one other time before this night but that was when he and I broke up for three days a few months ago or some shit like that.  He also added that he used a condom with her, which I knew was a lie for sure, since he just came out and volunteered that information for free.  Benji was never a big fan of contraceptives. Hell, we only used a condom the 1st time we were together and have never used them again...ever! And keep in mind; he does have 4 other kids already with various women.  So you must know that he and the Trojan Man really ain't too cool.

After what seemed like hours of his explaining, apologizing and confessions of his love for me, I was basically laying there on the bed numb. He was laying on top of me breathing his Hennessy mixed with Black N' Mild breath in my face. I didn't have the energy to keep arguing and struggling and I didn't have the energy to even try and leave anymore; my mind was gone and I just wanted to sleep at that point.

He kept kissing me and rubbing my hair, while he took my Bebe rhinestone printed top and my jeans off. He then put my limp, lifeless body, with my black Victoria Secret's bra and panty set on, under the covers and told me that he had to go make that money. He promised me things like that wouldn't happen anymore and that I should just rest, he would make it up to me. He tried to make a joke about the fact that he didn't know how strong I was when I broke out the back window of his truck with one swing. He said that he was going to take the cost of replacing the window out of my shopping allowance and then he laughed to himself. I know he was still high as a Chesapeake kite and not making any sense anyways. I had no more words, no more tears; I just closed my eyes and decided to deal with all this shit in the morning and so I went to sleep.

When I woke up the next morning, around 11:00am, it was to the sound of "Forever My Lady", by Jodeci, blaring from the stereo in the den downstairs; it just kept repeating over and over. I just figured Benji was down there tripping and still on his cocaine binge from the night before.

Oh, just in case you are not familiar with the effects of cocaine, let me explain. When a person is high off coke, they don't usually sleep until they come all the way down off of it. So they could stay up for days as long as they keep doing it and keeping their high. Believe me there has been many a night that the sun has caught the both of us over and over again. But that day I wasn't high, I was still mad as hell and feeling very worthless and confused.

I sat up in the bed and looked around at what a mess the room was in from our scuffle the night before. I looked over at my duffle bag laying on the floor with some of my clothes in it and the rest of my clothes scattered all over the room. I got up and walked over to the bag and began to pick up my clothes and put them back in the bag, still unsure of what I was planning to do.

As I walked past the dresser, I stopped and looked in the mirror and realized it was cracked. I didn't even remember breaking that mirror last night because I was in such a rage. But once I saw that mirror, that's when I decided that I was still going to leave... I had to leave. In my eyes, that cracked mirror represented this raggedy ass relationship and the seven years of bad luck that probably was to follow if I remained in it. I wasn't going to be that dumb chick that I always talked so badly about. You know the one that took any kind of treatment from her man until it beat her down to nothing. Or could I have possibly already been at that point?

As I was packing up, I looked up and saw Benji standing in the doorway of our bedroom, with a ridiculous smile on his face. He was still looking like last night with the same clothes on and smelling even worse than he did hours earlier.  I just rolled my eyes and kept doing what I was doing.  He stopped me as I was walking into the closet; he grabbed my hand and turned me to face him.

All the while that damn Jodeci song was still playing downstairs. I looked up at him like he was stupid and then he dropped down to one knee and took my left hand in his. He looked me straight in my Chinese eyes, and he said "Yana, I know things haven't always been perfect between us and you have stuck by my side through all of my shit. But you are my Yana, my baby and no matter what I have done in the past, just know that at the end of the day, I do love you so much and you can't be replaced."

I was staring at him in disgust and I said," You must think I am the dumbest bitch in the world to go for that simple shit you just said. I am done Benji, it's over, and I'm leaving! I'm so sick and so tired of how you do me. You don't know the meaning of love, you are nasty and trifling as hell and you only think about getting some ass!"

I tried to pull my hand away, but he just squeezed harder and he said, "Yana, things are about to be really different with us, I'm going to change. I'm done with all those tricks in the streets, for real! Don't you remember that song that's playing downstairs? That's the song we danced to when I first felt on your phat ass, baby." He laughed at his stupid little comment, but I was still with the blank stare.

I said, "You are a fool, let go of my hand! And why are you on the floor? You must be extra high off some real powerful shit this morning. Just leave me alone and let me pack my things and get the hell out of here!"

At that moment he reached in the left pocket of his Red Monkey jeans and pulled out a light blue box and held it up to my face. He then let go of my hand and I was stuck there just staring at him while still feeling like the dumbest chick on earth and in a daze by everything that was going on.

He then pulled out a $44 thousand, 2 carat platinum, emerald cut Legacy style ring with the bead set diamonds on the sides from Tiffany's. He then took my left hand again and slid that ring on my size 7 ring finger with my freshly done French manicure.  Then he said, "I want you with me forever Yana, I love you and I need you! Plus, I done got so used to your little monkey toes and how they scratch my legs up at night, I just can't live without that shit now. So you wanna do this thing right and marry your nigga or what?"

I just starred right into his eyes as my vision was beginning to blur from the tears welling up in my own eyes. I gave him a side smirk and then the tears just started streaming down my face. I started crying so hard and laughing at the same time from the mixed emotions and the mood of that moment, not to mention that off the wall comment about my toes that he made towards the end of the proposal. WTF? I was so overwhelmed because this was the ring that I had picked out when we were in the Tiffany store at South Park Mall about 6 months before that. I wasn't expecting this in a million years; I didn't even think he was really listening to me that day in the store. Evidently, he *was* paying attention.

I couldn't seem to take my eyes off of him. I was trying to feel the sincerity of his words through his eyes since he doesn't express himself verbally too often. I just thought if I looked deep enough into his pupils that it would be revealed to me that he was for real and meant all of this. I felt so torn, because on one hand he had never gone this far in apologizing before and then on the other hand I felt that what he told me about that girl Sparkle was all a big fat lie and he wasn't ever going to change. I just wasn't sure.

However, I just couldn't say no with all that bling, blinding me all up in my face. After all, I figured this was the pot of gold or should I say the pot of platinum that I had been hanging in there for all this time. So, I shook my head in a yes motion and we just held each other and listened to KC and JoJo sing the song a few times more.

I'm sure most of you would not have believed what he said to me or that he was for real. However, I had to have some faith in him. But let me elaborate a little more on my man, so perhaps you will have a deeper understanding of him and why it's so hard to let go.

Remember the monkey toe comment that he made when he was proposing to me? That is actually typical of Benji. He is always saying something crazy to make me laugh which is what I find most endearing about him. He is such a character and really funny, he should have been a comedian or something. I love laughing and normally I can't stay mad at him because he knows exactly what to say to get a chuckle or a smile out of me.

He always says such off the wall sayings and he cracks jokes on everybody at the most inappropriate times. Whereas most people see him as this hardcore street dude with a short temper that flips his wig all the time, in actuality he has such a witty sense of humor that he will have your sides hurting from the jokes. He's really unpredictable, so I'm always on my toes with him. Just when you think he will get mad about something that's when he won't and then vice versa. But his temperament also has a lot to do with the lifestyle he leads, the shady people he deals with daily, and let's not forget his drug indulgences that keep his moods swinging from right to left.

Even with all that said, bottom line is that I love Benji with all my heart and although he has his jacked up ways, this is the life I chose. I guess maybe I feel if he is taking this step towards marriage, that he will take other steps too. Maybe he will get out the game, give up the drugs, all the women and just focus on us. Just maybe this is the start for him to do something else for our future rather than sticking to this street hustle plan that he thinks is so great.

Don't get me wrong, when I think back on that whole ordeal from last year, I still sometimes wonder what would have happened if I did leave. What would my life be like now? Could that have been my wakeup call of what type of person I was dealing with or was that just a test of our love? In either case, that was a year ago and now our wedding is right around the corner so I guess I will never know that answer... because I chose to stay.

The wedding planning started immediately and he told me that I had full control. So when he told me that, he had to know I was going to break his pockets. I was going to do it big, if not for nothing but just on the principle of the lie he told me on the night before he proposed.

So, I know you recall the stripper, Sparkle, the one that I caught him with last year? Okay, well remember he told me that she wasn't pregnant by him because they only had sex twice. The one time when he supposedly used the condom and the second time was the night I caught him with her in the truck. He said that he didn't even get to "finish" that night because of my inconvenient interruption, yeah right? Well, truth be told, six months later and after a DNA test confirmed that the little girl was 99.9% his, all he could say was," Baby, I swear the condom must have broken."

As I mentioned earlier, Sparkle is officially his 4th baby mama, and she has his 5th child. So I figure since this dude has put me through having yet another child while we been together and we still don't have one of our own; everybody was going to know that he has chosen me above any other chicken head or baby mama and he put a ring on it.

I want all the various birds, baby mamas, haters and the whole world to know that Ayana

Dubois (soon to be Mrs. Sykes, if your nasty), made it through the storm with this dude and he is mine, on paper… in black and white. So now all the bitches need to back off, well at least that's how I hope it will be.

Benji knows that marriage is the real deal for me, it's a real serious thing, and the boyfriend/girlfriend playtime is OVER! He always said that he was only going to be married once and that's it for him so he chose me to do that with. All in all we have the same views on true commitment and that's why I believe that he is finally done with all the excess women and bullshit that he used to do out there in the streets.

I mean don't you think if Benji still planned to do like he had been doing me all these years, he wouldn't be going through all this trouble to marry me? I have faith in my man and I feel this is a stepping stone for better things to come. Right?

## CHAPTER THREE

Today seemed to be a beautiful Sunday autumn afternoon here in the Queen City, that's the nickname for the city of Charlotte. Despite all my mama's phone interruptions; I was about to get things together for my bachelorette party that was planned for the following week. I was waiting on my sister, Tiana and my home girl, Jazz to come over to help me plan for it.

I know customarily that the bachelorette party should be handled by them alone and I should be surprised and all, but hell, I'm the one getting married.  So my input and my ideas of what I want, have to be up in the mix too.  Jazz can be a little bit ghetto fabulous at times and my sister is just plain off the hook. So if I wanted some class then I had to make sure my girl's did this thing right.

I was sitting in my gorgeous new rattan patio chair in my sunroom in our brand new 5000 square foot home that sits on 13 acres of land. I was having an afternoon drink, my favorite, Ocean Spray Cran Apple juice mixed with Grey Goose, smoking on a Newport Light cigarette with my feet propped up on the foot stool, just chilling and relaxing.

We just moved into this house on the northwest side of town, not too far off highway 16, a few months ago.  Benji had it built from scratch. He said he didn't want his wife to live anywhere anyone else had lived, so he designed it all himself. It is a 3 level, 5 bedroom brick home with 4 garages, a pool and a movie theatre. It is basically furnished with Italian designer furniture and the best granite countertops and expensive marble floors, but we are still in the process of doing some last minute decorating. It's our first house that's this large and it has an outdoor Jacuzzi attached to the pool, so we can throw some real nice grown and sexy parties out here next summer.  I really love my new house, it's like a palace and I am feeling just like the queen I was born to be.

We have always had luxury items, but within the last 3 to 4 years or so, things have really stepped up to the next level for us. Benji has begun to invest in some legitimate businesses, thanks to my collegiate input trying to make him see a bigger picture outside of hustle life.

His investments are on a small level right now, but if he is ever to get out of this drug life, he has to start somewhere. He recently put in some funds with his boy, Clutch, on a couple urban clothing stores that he opened off Albemarle Road and he has another one opening up next week in the University area. They sell all the latest name brands that black folks like to see branded all over their outfits to let everyone know how much cash they are sporting around on their bodies. Meanwhile, the majority of them are probably still living at home with their mama in the projects, driving the latest whips, not working and hanging out at the club frontin' every weekend. It's sad, but for some reason that way of life becomes the norm to some of "our people".

Anyways, I have been telling him to try and get into the real estate game in order to make everything legit, so he wouldn't have to hustle at all anymore. The amount of money that can be made in housing is crazy, we could still live good and he could stop risking his life out here in these streets. He says, he will think about it and look into it, but I believe that Benji actually likes the thrill of the streets and everything that comes with it. This is what he has known since he was 14 years old and I think he's afraid to do something different because he is unfamiliar with it.

I can't really complain about anything too much though, most women would kill to be in my place, and actually they have tried. There is a lot that Benji doesn't always tell me about though. Such as how we acquire all of the things that we have, such as the cars, the homes, the motorcycles, etc., all the stuff that has to be signed for in someone's name. He says that it's better if I don't know everything that goes on in his business. I am not real sure who it was better for though, if it was for him or for me?

None of our property was in either of our names. He said it was for security reasons, because of what he does for a living and obviously the extravagance of how we live. Since he doesn't like to pay a whole lot of miscellaneous bills every month, he always pays everything a few months ahead or just pays it close to paid in full if possible. I never see bills coming to the house. So whoever's name all our stuff is in is getting a hell of a great FICO score.

The only thing that was in my name was the car insurance. In the back of my mind, I would think about if I ever was to be apart from him, I have absolutely no credit in my name. I've been with him and living off of his means for 14 plus years, so I would be stuck and would have to rely on any savings that I had accumulated from him. It is all so overwhelming that I often try not to think about it at all.

Benji likes to be seen and he is often in the hot spots around town and loves to be very flashy with what he has. Because of this Charlotte's Finest in blue and white are always keeping an eye on him, along with all the haters that act like they down with him, but in reality they want to cut his throat and take what he has at any minute. So for that reason, before we go home every day, we have to check and recheck for followers. It's a must to take all kinds of different crazy routes to the house to make sure no one finds out where the crib is, we don't want to get robbed or busted. You may think, damn, that is so extra to have to do on a daily basis just to go home. But hey, that's just part of this lifestyle and so I do what is necessary and I just enjoy the fruits of it all.

Did I mention my brand new 2006 Metallic black BMW 750li with the custom rims, this new house, our summer condo in Miami, the extravagant furniture, etc. , that is just some of what he supplies me with for all the drama that I have to endure. I did hear him mention to one of his boys' that this house cost somewhere in the ballpark of $750,000 and I believe he paid a good portion of that off before we even moved in.  So living like I do, I really don't ask too many questions of him about our things. Besides, his arrogant ass wouldn't tell me the truth and then he would tell me to shut up and enjoy it, so that's what I do!

While I am waiting for Tiana and Jazz to come to the house to get my party organized, I just happened to gaze out at the backyard from the sunroom and noticed the beauty of nature and how the leaves were beginning to fall off the trees. I saw a squirrel eating a nut off the ground and I was able to smell the fresh fragrance of the autumn grass that came from the wind hitting off the pond we have in the back.  At that moment I began to think of how simple life is for that little squirrel, all he has to worry about is not running out in front of a car at the wrong time and getting splattered.

But for the 1st time in my life or at least in a really long time, I stopped to notice normal things that occur around me every day that I'm usually too busy to recognize. I started thinking what it could be like if I had a normal existence, I mean a normal life with normal people in it. Like people who do stuff like take walks in the park and plant flowers in the garden and notice squirrels eating nuts and just regular shit.

Just then Claire and Cliff came to mind; don't front! You know if you grew up in the 80's, the Huxtables were the bomb family. We all wanted to be one of their kids or at least one of their kids' friends that got to go over to their house. I mean I was thinking they had money and nice things just like Benji and I do. Difference is they both went to a job every day and raised their kids with good values and everyone around them talked with sense and respected each other. They didn't go around, saying words like "bitch, hoe, trick, nigga and all that shit", like I hear and use in my daily circle. Their life seemed so peaceful and deep down that's what I truly longed for...normalcy.

Although I am half way there to Cosby life since I am about to be married, Benji and I don't have any kids of our own yet. So I guess that's good we are starting with marriage first and THEN the kids will come later. But I still have to deal with the excessive weight and baggage of the 5 kids that he already has and that they are coming into our new life together. Don't get me wrong, I like his kids, even though they are bad as hell. They have nothing to do with how they got here and the circumstances they were born into. But at that moment, the reality of me never being able to have that fairy tale family like I dreamed of, hit me like a brick. Truth is, I can never be Claire, because Cliff aka Benji already has all five of the Cosby kids: Sondra, Denise, Theo, Vanessa, Rudy better known to him as TaTa, Shaquana and Daquan, the twins, Nyami and Lanisha, by those four other women.

I am always going to have to deal with a baby mama and some kid running around my house that looks nothing like me. I also have to think that if and when we have our own children, will he make my experience any less, because this isn't his first? Yes, of course I knew all of this when I said yes to him.

But since the time of the wedding was coming closer, I guess I was getting a little more apprehensive about my future and my true happiness.

As I was watched that little squirrel run up the tree and eat his nut, I thought even more about my career. I wasn't currently working because Benji said that I didn't need to with all the money he makes for us. Even though he did put me through four years of college at North Carolina A&T State University, where I earned a bachelor's degree in Theatre- Performance Arts, he didn't really like me to go on auditions or anything that would take away from me being home. He said as long as he had a clean house, cooked food when he wanted to eat and I gave him some ass whenever he wanted it, then he would always take care of me. He said I could always "act" for him in the bedroom, if I wanted to act and that me becoming famous was just a silly dream.

He would tell me that this hustle life is what's for real and what keeps us eating and living good. But something in me just feels a need for more, like I need my own identity. I sometimes wonder if once we get married will Benji be more supportive of my acting or will he get worse?

All this nature watching was starting to bug me out and make my mind go crazy, so I decided to get my ass up and leave the sunroom. I was going to go into the TV room to watch Busta Rhyme's countdown on BET with the half-naked booty shaking girls in the videos on the plasma screen. I mean, this right here is the atmosphere that I am accustomed to. I must be crazy to have second thoughts about my life, I'm truly living the glamorous life, and I got it made. Why would I be thinking about corny shit like squirrels, grass and gardens? I must have been tripping off a drug after effect.

So now with my mind focused on this video trash, I won't be thinking about all that Discovery Channel shit. I feel my thoughts are much safer in this room listening to meaningless rap lyrics and strip club beats while I am waiting for Tiana and Jazz.

Jazz is my matron of honor, since she is technically the married one and Tiana, my little sister, is going to be my maid of honor. But, if my marriage turns out anything like Jazz's then I might as well not even do this damn thing.

Jazz is my home girl, Jasmine, is her real name and we have been tight ever since college. She is originally from Charlotte and she moved back here after she got pregnant in our junior year. She got married about two years later and she never came back to school because she kept having babies.

I call her Lightbright, because she looks almost like a white girl. If it wasn't for her blond hair being nappy as a sheep's ass and that little pug nose of hers, you would never know that she had any part of Kunta Kente in her blood. She is a spunky person, about 5'5 and a little thick in the middle with these little skinny chicken legs. She used to be real skinny when we were in college, before she started having all those damn babies.

Even though she is light skinned, please don't get it twisted. As soon as Ms. Jazz opens her mouth, you know she is straight representing for the Westside, she's a definite sista!

She is very pro black, and since college she has always been so fascinated with Africa, West Indies and the civil rights movement. When we were in school, she was in the Pan African History club which supported rallies to uplift the African American movement and all that kind of stuff. So regardless of the fact that she's from the hood and never graduated college, she is very intelligent and she keeps herself up to speed on what is going on in the black community. She even teaches her kids all that historical stuff. I guess that's why she married the blackest man she could find, Norman, to make sure her babies came out showing more of their black heritage than she did.

But, as far as her marriage, you would never know she was married, if you didn't actually attend the wedding for yourself. She is always by herself with all those damn kids, 4 to be exact.  Her husband Norman, is only God knows where all the time; probably out at the bar and making more babies all over the place.  But hey, that's her life and she acts like she is happy with it, so that's on her to deal with it.  We all have our own bridges to cross. She's my girl no matter what and I will always have her back.

But wait, I know what you are saying; my man, Benji, has a lot of kids all over the place too.

But the difference is, that he didn't knock *me* up 4 times and leave me to go out and make more. Let's remember the key factor in all of this... my man has plenty money, which makes a huge difference! Benji also has straightened up and hasn't had any more babies since we've been engaged. So my situation isn't the same as hers, her man can barely take care of his family much less all the rest of them chaps he has all over Charlotte and Rock Hill, SC, where he's from. So, that makes a big difference, don't you think? Money always makes a difference, doesn't it?

Maybe it wouldn't be so bad for her, if she didn't have to work 2 jobs to keep their family together, when he only works one and that's when he decides to go to it. He calls himself trying to do some drug business with Benji from time to time. But that never seems to work out, because he winds up messing up the money some kind of way and Benji be wanting to kill him. Everybody can't be in the dope game and hustle; some people just aren't built for that life. So I do help her out with cash for the kids sometimes, but I try not to make a habit out of it. Because in reality, I know she will give it to Norman and that defeats the purpose.

Tiana is supposed to be picking up Jazz from her weekend job at the Nine West store, in Carolina Place Mall and coming over. If Jazz went home first she would get stuck there.  Norman, never wants her to go anywhere, but to and from work and then back home and sit there like an idiot with those kids while he goes hanging out all night. So today, we had to detour all of that nonsense.

Unfortunately, Tiana doesn't know the meaning of time; so of course they were running late. But, that's my sister and I am very much used to her slack, inconsiderate ways.  She was probably being held up by her sorry excuse of a man, Chucky.  She was most likely waiting at her house for him to bring her car back to her, so she could leave.  Yes, I said HER car! Knowing his trifling self, he probably hasn't even been home since the night before, but that's the norm.  My sister put up with so much useless shit from that no good dude; it was simply a waste of time.

Tiana is a beautiful, caramel toned, petite framed little lady with a set of double DD's and a cute little booty to set it off.  She has a little bit of a pudgy tummy now, ever since she had my 18 month old nephew, Austin, but she's still straight.

On the real, I have seen non-pregnant chicks who look 10 months pregnant every day.  Their body's all jacked up, stretched marked out and looking like Flava Flav in the face but they will at least have a man with some benefits and their own car.  For most dudes, it really doesn't matter in this day and time what a female's body looks like as long as she is giving up some booty, most dudes will hit it and at times even make her wifey is she is taking care of him.  What in the hell is up with that?  What about all the single sista's hitting the gym and keeping their bodies tight? Where is the love?

Anyways, I said all that to say, that I know my sister is way too fine for that pathetic piece of a man that she has. I really can't stand him, because he doesn't do anything positive for my sister. He more or less lives off of her and stresses her out rather than helping her move up in life. I know he probably smacks her around too, I have seen marks on her. She would never tell me if he has hit her because she knows I would have one of Benji's boys jack him up something serious. I don't understand it, but for some strange reason she loves that little snaggle toothed troll.  But I can't be worried about her all the time, she's a grown woman and I can't make her see what he is about if she doesn't want better for herself.

I looked up at the clock on the wall, it read 1:30pm and I realized Benji was still in the bed which was normal because it is still a little early for him to be up and about on a Saturday. I knew I had to get up today and get together with my girl's early, so I didn't go and hang out with him at the club last night. Normally, I would still be in the bed too, but someone has to be the responsible one in this relationship and get this wedding together. To be real, if it wasn't for me this wedding would be taking place downtown at the justice of the peace. His homeboy Freeze as our witness, followed up by a trip to Atlantic City to gamble our entire honeymoon away. I said no way; I wasn't going to let it go down like that, so I have taken full charge of everything. He hasn't put too much input into at all besides the money.

I just tell him how much I need in order to pay for things and he says something like, "Damn, Yana, what the hell is that shit for? Do we really need it? Or is that just some bourgeois shit YOU want?" I then give him this look that mentally says," Nigga, you got that trick pregnant when we were together and I'm still wit yo' triflin ass!" and then he just reaches into his pocket and hands over the cash.

Matter of fact, this entire wedding has been paid for with cash, we don't use credit cards. Benji says credit cards are for people who want to act like they have money. But you know you are a true baller if you can pay cash for everything you buy. But since most transactions in the business world require credit to reserve things, I had to get my mother to reserve our honeymoon package to Trinidad and the reception hall on her credit card.

I guess I'm good with how I am in control of all the arrangements, but it would be kind of nice if Benji was a little more involved. But that's just him, he is who he is, so I either deal with it or I don't. I've been dealing with it so long, that I'm just used to the shit now.

Don't get it twisted...just because he's not helping me with planning this wedding; I know Benji loves me, and he shows it in his own way. It's usually with money and great sex that has me speaking in tongues, so I won't complain. I mean even after all the years and all the fucked up things that he has put me through, when we get it on in the bed, it's still like when we first started dating. To be honest, I think this dude put a root on me or something. I probably should have left him years ago way before the Sparkle incident ever happened, but where would I go? This life is all I know.

# CHAPTER FOUR

I am sure you may be wondering, how did a girl from the bitter cold city in the Midwest, Minneapolis, Minnesota end up living my life like the black Gotti's, in North Carolina. As I am still waiting on my sister and Jazz I will tell you. Well, it was about 15 years ago and the simplistic life in Minneapolis was changing drastically. A lot of gangs from Chicago and Detroit had moved in to the city and my mother, being a single a mother said she didn't want me and my sister to get caught up in a lot of the crazy street activity that was going on there. Translation: she didn't want us to get knocked up by a thug ass dude and get trapped in Minneapolis not doing anything with our lives.

My mother always wanted better for us, so we went to private Catholic schools all our lives, where the population was only about 2% black. She had hopes of providing us with greater opportunities for our future than she had.  We were in no way rich growing up, but my mother worked very hard to make sure we lived decently in a middle class neighborhood and we had what we needed.

Although, my mom used to work long hours, she was always supportive of our dreams. I always wanted to become a big movie star like Diana Ross in Lady Sings the Blues. She used to tell me that I was made for the movies because I was always so dramatic and putting on a show.

Tiana, was the one who always had to have the last word on everything and she wanted to be a big time trial lawyer. With that mouth of hers, she could definitely work it out in the courtroom. Yes, we both had our big dreams and mom raised us with strong minds and the confidence to accomplish whatever we desired to do in life.

So she sent both of us to live with her sister, Tammy, and her son, my cousin, Terrance, down in

Greensboro, NC. Tiana was going to finish up high school down there and I was going to enroll in college. My mom preferred for me to attend a university such as, Duke or Carolina, because I had the grades to get in either of them. She knew they were both great schools for better career opportunities.

But once we moved to NC, I had already decided that I wanted to attend an HBCU and my aunt, Tammy agreed that I should; she felt that I needed to get more in touch with "my people". She always thought my mom was raising us to be "too white" and that we needed to get some of our own culture instilled in us.

I think my mom was just trying to raise us different than she was raised. Is there anything wrong with a parent wanting more for their children than they had for themselves? It just so happens to be that statistically, predominately white schools provide a better education for all students from what I heard. As far as I'm concerned, my mom's method of raising us was actually selfless and that's why I do all that I can do for her to this day.

Aunt Tammy was always concerned that we would get beat down in an alley or something because we acted like white girls and couldn't fight. But Aunt Tammy didn't know how gangster I really was and that when I was in 5th grade, I did have a fight. I punched this bully named Deon from the neighborhood, blacked his eye, right in the hallway of his own apartment building. Now you know that's straight hood to beat somebody's ass at their own crib! LOL!

He had pushed Tiana off her bike and made her bust her knee on the concrete. No one messed with my baby sister and got away with it.  So little did auntie know I do have street cred, at least by my own pitiful stats; I have 1 knockout and no losses.

Shit, I should get double props for that win because Deon was older, in the 6$^{th}$ grade and he was a boy.

Anyways, when we got to NC with Aunt Tammy, we moved into a predominately black neighborhood. I do admit we were a bit naïve and sheltered but I think we adjusted well.

The first year we were there I worked at the Four Seasons mall in the Express store, so I could gain NC residency and avoid having to pay the out-of-state tuition for college.  Tiana was a sophomore when we moved there and she went to Dudley High School, not the most hood school, but had its fair share of black folks.  Tiana loved it and jumped into her new environment head first, it was like she was straight out of Brooklyn or something, but with a country twist.

Okay, so there you have it, that's the story of how I wound up living in NC. As far as Benji and I getting together, I met him about 3 months after I moved down here and my cousin Terrance took me to this party at the National Guard Armory. The Armory was a spot that hosted special events, it was about 15 minutes from the college campus but it was a neighborhood spot, so usually just the local Greensboro kids partied there. Mad Lion, the reggae hip hop artist was performing there that night, so we had to check it out.

Terrance was a real cool dude, he was country as hell but he knew everybody around town. He had been in Greensboro since he was five years old. Aunt Tammy moved down here when Terrance's dad got a job transfer out of Minneapolis to Greensboro. They liked it down south so much, they never left. Terrance's dad died when he was 12 years old from lung cancer and he and Aunt Tammy became just like best friends, he truly stayed strong for his mama. He's a real good guy with no drama and has a good job at Lorillard, the local tobacco plant. Which

I find is ironic since his dad died from smoking cigarettes. But hey, a job is a job, right?

Okay, back to the party. We were chillin' at the spot and Terrance was taking me all around, introducing me to all his friends. I felt all eyes on me , probably because I had on my red Cross Colors oversized t-shirt and my black Cross Colors long baggy shorts with the my red, black and green cloth belt on that Aunt Tammy let me borrow. My hair was in a French roll with spiral curls hanging down in the front. I thought I looked hot! Trust me, you couldn't tell me that I wasn't the shit, remember that was the 90's and I thought I was actually in style with all that Cross Colors mess on.

Terrance knew all types of people. The drug boys, the hot chicks, the weed heads, the dance crews, just everybody. But he didn't cling to one particular group, he did his own thing and they all seemed to be cool with him.

When he introduced me to Benji, all these girls were flocked around him and he just looked at me and laughed. I looked at him and said, "What the hell is so funny?" He said, "Where you from Shawty?"

I said, "Minnesota!"

He said, "Minna –What?" Where the hell is dat? Near Idaho or something?"

I replied," No smart ass, it's near North Dakota and Wisconsin. Why? What difference does it make?"

Benji says, with a smirk on his face, "Well you and that outfit need to go back to Minnetonka because down here we stopped wearing that Cross Colors shit over a year ago. You rocking it like you just pulled it off the store shelf. It's all crisp and fresh and shit!"

And then everyone started cracking up. I was so mad and embarrassed. I was thinking that I wanted to crawl under a rock and just stay there until the party was over.  How dare this dude talk to me like that, he didn't even know me.

I just looked at Terrance and asked him what was up with that asshole and was all of his friends that rude? Terrance told Benji that he was wrong for that and we walked off to the other side of the room.

Later on Benji walked over to me and apologized. He said that he thought I was a cutie and he just didn't want me to look crazy now that I'm in his town.  I must admit even though he made me feel like a total fool, he was so fine; I couldn't resist talking to him. We talked all the way through the Mad Lion performance and I couldn't help but notice all the girls just looking at us and whispering, obvious hating going on.

Once the party started to wind down, the dj played slow jams and when "Forever My Lady", by Jodeci came on, he asked me to dance with him.  He was too cool of a guy to have danced to all that fast music; he liked this grinding type of music better. From that point he glued his hands to my butt and got in a couple squeezes that I pretended bothered me, but really it didn't.

It was like we were the only two people in the place. He smelled so good and I had my face was buried in his nicely defined chest with his Polo cologne immersed in the cloth of his Girbaud striped button up shirt. Everything was going good, until a fight broke out and then the sound of gun shots rang out inside the building. These were the pre-mandatory metal detector days.

Benji pushed me away and ran off somewhere and I was left standing in the middle of the floor like a bald chicken. Then Terrance came running up beside me and grabbed me by the arm and pulled me in the direction of the entrance out of the building. There was a stampede of kids running out with us, everyone in a chaotic frenzy. Who would have thought this little country ass town of Greensboro would have all this action going on?  But it was kind of exciting but scary at the same time.

Once we got out to the parking lot, panting and checking for bullet wounds, we started laughing at how crazy that was.  Everybody just started hanging out in the parking lot, playing their car stereos like none of that madness just happened.  I was amazed.

Terrance and I were walking back to his car and then I heard my name being called. "Yana!", "Yana!" a deep manly voice called out.  I stopped walking and turned around to see that it was Benji approaching me with some speed.

He said that he apologized for pushing me away, but it was some of his people that were engaged in that fight, so he had to go and handle the situation. He asked if he could get my number and take me out sometime.  I was about to play hard to get...but for what? I wanted to give him my number when we were in the party and plus the police were pulling into the parking lot, so there was no time for all that dramatic play with the boy. So I gave him Aunt Tammy's number and he said he would call me the next day.

The next day came and he called and we went out. We have been going out, falling out, breaking up, making up, moving in, moving out, going through good times and bad times ever since. It's almost fifteen years later and now this man and I are getting married in two weeks. You can almost say that we grew up together; we have been through so much. Life is so funny sometimes; you just never know what you will end up with from an initial encounter with someone.

## CHAPTER FIVE

The doorbell finally rings.  It's about time these slow chicks got here.  I walk out to the atrium and opened the door. I look into my little sister's smiling face, grinning ear to ear and she says giggling, "Damn, bitch, you just sittin' around in this big ole' house like you Paris Hilton or something?  I'm surprised you don't have a butler like Mr. Bentley to answer your damn door!"

"Shut the hell up Tiana! You so stupid just get your ass in here" I said, as I stepped aside so she could step up into the atrium.

"Girl, you know we gotta have a party up in this piece!" This house is crucial! Y'all must be slinging some boatloads of coke these days to afford this shit," Jazz says as she follows in behind Tiana.

"Both of you have no sense.  But I am glad you slow bitches finally made it here before it got dark. Damn, what took y'all so long?" I said.

Jazz replies, "Bitch, you know how they are at the store and they don't want to let me leave until, THEY are ready to let me leave. Them silly white hoes in that store make me sick. I'm fixin' to quit that job anyways."

I said, "Again Jazz?  Is Norman working steady now?"

"Well, He..." she began to say.

"Never mind honey, I don't even want to go there today.  It's my bachelorette party planning day. Let me show y'all chickens around the house first." I said with excitement.

Tiana said, "We can look around on our own. This isn't Buckhead Palace or whatever the hell it's called; we don't need an official tour by you Ms. Thang!"

I laughed as they proceeded to walk to the kitchen area and I said, "Fine then bitches, don't ask no questions about nothing either.  When y'all are done, I'm gonna take y'all down to the waterfront for a seafood lunch and we can talk about the plans there."

Jazz says in a slave type voice, "Okay Boss lady, fo sho, we's a gonna do whatever you a tell us to do, it's yo day!" They laughed together as they walked out of sight.

I went back into the TV room to turn off the television and to look for my cigarettes. I picked up my pack of cigarettes and pulled one out and lighted up. I figured I should go upstairs and tell my baby, Benji that we were gonna be leaving.

So as the girls were still wandering around downstairs, I heard them outside on the deck chit chatting about the hot tub. Of course they were cracking jokes the whole time about how Benji and I think we are living the life of royalty. I know my girls are happy for me, hopefully they are not jealous and the happiness is genuine. But you know how sistas can be!  Smile in your face and then wanting

to snatch your weave off you're your head as soon

as you turn your back.  In either case, they know all

that I have endured to get to this point, so screw

them if they *are* hating on me.

As I approached our bedroom, I heard the

rumbling of Benji snoring like a wildebeest. So I

knew that if I woke him up to tell him that I was

going out, he probably wouldn't even remember.  I

know he was not going to wake up until about 4 or 5

pm anyways.  I think I heard him come in about 5am

this morning.  So I know he was out last night

getting high and doing business, probably gambling.

That was one of his hustle gigs too.

He would go to the gambling houses and play

poker with the big dogs when he was feeling lucky.

They would play like $1000 hands at the table in the

front of the house and for lesser amounts throughout

the rooms going towards the back of the house.

These gambling spots were illegal, of course and they were run by white folks, real important people in the community.

You would have to know somebody and get invited to be able to attend and play. I went with Benji a few times and it was like a scene straight out of Casino or something. The building would look like a regular business building or a really big house in a business area. They would have surveillance cameras all around the building and you would have to knock and know a code word to say to get in. When they opened the door it was usually a small little white lady and a country looking white dude with a rifle in hand and they would have to raise up this big metal bolt thing and let you in past the metal detector. Real gangsta type shit!

Once you got in they were overly nice to you and there would be chicks in the kitchen cooking up all kinds of food, plenty of free drinks, snacks, rooms for people who smoke to chill in and TV rooms where you can watch satellite TV.  It was cool, but I would get bored quick, since I don't know how to gamble and cards don't really interest me in the first place. However, I figured that's what he had been doing last night, because when I looked on the floor at his shoe, he had several 100 dollar bills laying in the bottom of the shoe.

He would put money in his shoe like that, when he played cards so that he wouldn't spend all of his money, in case he was losing.  Since he would usually get drunk at the gambling house, he would most likely forget that he even had the money in his shoe. So when he was tapped out from spending what he had on him, he would leave and realize the next morning that he didn't lose everything.  Benji couldn't stand being empty handed when he was out, so that was his whacky strategy for not going flat broke when he played cards.

Anyways, I picked up his Evisu jeans that were hanging over the chair to check and see if he had any money left. And when I reached into the pocket, he actually had about $4000, so last night was a good night for him. All I could do was to smile as I looked at my man, lying on the bed on his stomach with half of his long body under the covers and his foot hanging off the side of the bed. I wanted so much more for his life than what he was doing, I mean what WE were doing. Yeah, we lived luxurious, but the risks and sacrifices that we had to deal with was always a daily stressor for me.

As I was going over to the dresser to splash on some Bvlgari perfume before I left out, I noticed his Treo cell phone flashing red on the nightstand. I normally don't pay any attention to his phone because he usually turns it off when he gets home. All those Negroes from the hood start calling him about getting some work early in the morning and he doesn't feel like the disturbances, so he just cuts off his phone when he comes home. I guess when he came in this morning he was a bit too wasted and forgot to turn it off.

So I picked it up to turn it off and when I looked at the screen it was a text message alert flashing. Benji doesn't even use text messaging with people except for when he is responding to me. He doesn't like pushing all those buttons, he prefers to pick up the phone and just say what he has to say.

I pushed the READ button and it was a message from a stored number with the name Syn. I don't know of any one of his boys named Syn, and when he is doing business with most people that he isn't really tight with, he doesn't lock their name in his phone.

So as I opened the text message it read: Baby, i know how much u love me.the way you fukd me last nite & this mornin,shows me. can't wait till our baby comes, we can b 2gether 4good. Luv u,Synthia.

"What in the hell?" I whispered to myself.  I am holding the phone in my hand and just staring at the words over and over, trying to make sure that I am really seeing what I am seeing.  I go to his message inbox and I see that there are 3 other messages in there from Syn dated last night.  So I read those too.

There was one sent to him at 6:02pm that read: Baby, I need $500 to get some more maternity clothes. I will be back home by 7pm.C u later.Luv u,Synthia.

The next one was sent at 8:37pm that read: Benji baby,I c u called me. Was in shower preparing for u 2 fuk me all nite.cum when u ready, u got the key.luv u Synthia.

The final one was sent at 10:04pm and it read: Babe, hope u didn't get stuck wit that bitch of yours

.u know u love my sweetness better.hurry up.the baby misses u.luv u Synthia.

I then scrolled through the outbox messages and it only had one message in it and what do you know, it was being sent at 10:43pm to Syn, it read:

b there in minute baby

I am feeling like I am in the Twilight Zone and that at any minute someone is going to pop out of my closet and say "April Fools Day" or "Gotcha" or something like that to deliver me from this hell.

"DAMN! DAMN! DAMN! This fucking dude did this shit to me again!" I said as I was squeezing the phone in my hand. I started chuckling to myself in a delusional daze, as I paced back and forth in front of the mirror, trying to figure out what I was going to do about this.

I thought of taking the .45 caliber out of the nightstand and sticking it in the back of his little pea head and blowing his brains out, but that would be a mess all over the room. Then I thought about taking

the cigarette that I was still holding in my left hand

that had just about burned into a line of ashes, and

burn holes all in his face. But that wasn't good

enough, he would wake up after the first burn, and I

wouldn't be able to finish mutilating him. Then I

thought about tying him up and setting him on fire,

but I couldn't do that either, that was too much work

and I don't think we had any lighter fluid or

whatever is needed to do a job like that.  Bottom line

is that all of those acts would send me straight to the

penitentiary and I am not built for a prison style

orange jumpsuit that is just not a good look for me.

So I looked in the mirror at myself and how

pretty I was. (Truth is it doesn't matter if you are

Halle Berry or Whoopi, men will still treat you like

shit if you let them!) I wasn't suffering from a coke

and liquor induced hang over this morning, so I

didn't have any bags under my eyes and I actually looked refreshed today.

I looked back through the mirror at Benji still lying on the bed in the same position. He had no worries in the world and that all was right with him, he was a perfect fiancé, as he had been portraying recently. He said he actually was ready to be serious and marry me. What a fucking joke, I thought! This man can't be good to anyone but himself, he will never get it together. In two weeks we are supposed to become one and he just stuck his penis in another woman last night and from what her text messages read, she is having HIS baby. I started laughing aloud although tears were streaming down my face, I couldn't' contain myself. I think I was going insane at that moment.

I dumped my cigarette in the ashtray on the dresser and I turned from the mirror and walked out of the bedroom into the hallway. I looked at his phone again and then pressed the talk button to call SYN. I wanted to hear what she had to say to the "bitch" as she referred to me in her text message.

As the phone rang, a woman answered with a very light squeaky voice, she said, "Hey my sexy man, what's up?"

I just held the phone to my ear for a moment without saying a word.

She said, "Baby, hello, can you hear me? Baby..."

I interrupted her and cleared my throat and replied, "This isn't Benji honey, this is Ayanna, his fiancé...Synthia?"

She started chuckling sarcastically and said. " Oh yeah, Ayanna, this is Synthia. But I don't think you're his fiancé! He never said that was who you were to him. But I guess he told you about me, huh?"

I stated firmly," No he didn't tell me anything bout your ass. I saw your text messages in his phone and I decided to call and see what is really good. He would never tell me about no other bitch. So you are supposed to be pregnant by him right? How long have you two been dealing with each other? Who did he tell you I was to him? I mean this shit is bugging me out for real. "

She said," I am 7 months pregnant and yes by Benji. We have been together for about 9 months. He pays all my bills and totally takes care of me, he loves me. We met at the mall, when I worked in the Nine West store. My coworker, his homegirl Jazz hooked us up. He says that he lets you live in his house cause you are his ex-girlfriend from a long time ago or something like that and he is just letting you get on your feet. He doesn't want you messing up all his business connects so he just puts up with your stupid ass until you get out."

"WOW! He said all that, huh? Well Miss Synthia, Benji and I are getting married in exactly two weeks and I have the diamonds on my finger to prove it. But you know what? I am not even going to go there with you. I actually believe what you are telling me. But please don't get it twisted, Benji is a chronic liar and I have been with him almost 15 years and I know him very well. So no matter what he tells you about me, it's only to tell you what you want to hear. And by the way, did he tell you that you will be his 5th baby mama? Yours will be number 6. How old are you anyways? You sound young." I asked shaking my head with amazement at the conversation that I was having with this naïve girl.

She replies with a quivering voice, "6 kids? What the hell? Are you sure? He told me this was his 2nd baby and that he was so excited to be having ours because it's a girl and his first one is a boy. He said that he can't wait and that he knows the baby is going to beautiful since I am from Ecuador. I'm 21 and he said that you would be gone once the baby was born. I don't believe any of this shit."

I guess I was so dazed that I didn't even notice her Spanish accent until after she told me that she was foreign. But the poor girl was just a boo hooing and snotting all into the phone that I kind of felt bad for her. Why would I feel bad for this trick, I don't know. I suppose it's because I made a choice to stay and deal with Benji knowing exactly who he is and what he is capable of. This young girl was bamboozled and misled into dealing with him. Now she is stuck with his trifling ass forever, because she's having his baby.

Although I could empathize with this chick, I had to deal with my own problems with this man. I told Synthia that she needs to get herself together and realize the type of man she is dealing with now and that he will only bring her down. I didn't want to talk to her anymore, I had heard enough. I told her thank you for the information and sorry that he lied to her, but that's just how Benji operates. I hit the END button on his phone, turned it off and then I threw it on the floor in the hallway.

I heard the girl's footsteps clicking around on the hardwood floor beneath me, they were still chit chatting and giggling with each other. All kinds of thoughts were racing through my mind about what to do next.  But what was sticking out the most was the fact that my girl, my home girl, Jasmine introduced this Jennifer Lopez bitch to my man.  I was bewildered and I was feeling so betrayed.

My mind was telling me to go up to Jazz and smack the hell out of her for hooking Benji up with this Synthia bitch and to ask her why in the hell she would do this to me.  But I felt crazy enough and all I wanted to do was to get the hell away from all these fucked up people who have apparently done me so wrong.

I could hear Jazz and Tiana making their way to the stairs, so I gathered my thoughts quickly and I walked back into the bedroom and grabbed 2 eight balls out of the top drawer, my purse and keys off the dresser. As I walked by the bed I looked across the room at my $10,000 2nd wedding dress (for the reception) hanging from my closet door and then I glanced at Benji's lifeless body sleeping so peaceful like he didn't have a care in the world. I couldn't help but hate him for what he has put me through and the thought of marrying this man made my stomach turn. That dress had as much meaning as a used condom to me. I was so over all this crap that I didn't even want to wake him up to discuss this shit, I just wanted to leave.

As I reached the doorway, the girls had made their way upstairs. They were looking at me, both of them with smiling faces unaware of my inner torment that just occurred.  I just looked at Jazz directly in the eyes with a look that could cut and automatically the tears began streaming down my face.  Tiana was reaching out to touch my arm and I pushed past her and I ran down the stairs and out the door.

I was walking as fast as I could to get in my car while Jazz and Tiana, were following close behind yelling my name. I was already in my car when I noticed that they were both at my window knocking and screaming "Yana, what's wrong? Yana, where are you going? What happened sis? Tell us! Yana!" That's all I heard as I drove away.  For all I know I could have run over one of those bitches feet, I have no idea; I was in a whirlwind with an objective of getting the hell out of there.

I drove down the Brookshire Freeway having no idea of a destination or a plan in mind.  All I had with me was my purse, a debit card, a pack of cigarettes, two eight balls of cocaine, the clothes on my back and my Giuseppe heels on my feet. But one thing I do know for sure is that if I didn't keep going down that road, my life would be over from a nervous breakdown or for killing Benji.  At that very moment I knew I would never go back to him, ever!

# CHAPTER SIX

I was still in a daze, but I couldn't help but notice that my phone was ringing off the hook with that damn "I'm Bossy" by Kelis, ring tone. I heard it going off in the background the entire time I was driving, but I think I finally snapped back into reality and I actually paid attention to it. I picked up the phone and I already knew what I was going to see even before I looked at it. A countless number of calls from Jazz and Tiana had filled up my call history on my phone log.

The little voicemail envelope was also lit up. I didn't even bother to listen to the voicemail messages; I didn't want to hear anything from them or even talk to either of them right now. I just turned the phone off.

I had to figure out where my destination would be. I was still just driving aimlessly and at this point I had merged onto I-77 South and I was already down near the Tyvola Road exit. I thought about going to my mother's house, but I knew she would rat me out because she can't hold water. So I got off on the Tyvola exit and drove all the way down the street when I realized that I was right in front of the South Park mall.

I went and parked in the Nordstrom's parking deck and I just sat in my car for what seemed like eternity and listened to my Anthony Hamilton cd play track number 3 over and over again. It was the song "Can't Let Go". I felt numb, embarrassed and so much anger, rage and hurt was racing through my mind. I am sure if anyone could see into my car through the limo tint, they would think I was a total nut job. I was crying and snorting and smoking cigarettes like I was on the chain gang. I was a complete mess!

As I got higher and higher I figured that I couldn't go into the mall in this condition, security would surely haul me off to Billingsley Mental Health. I glanced down at the clock on the dash and it read 9:02pm, the mall was closed anyways. I had been in this damn car for hours losing my fucking mind. I still didn't know where I was about to go. I looked over and saw the Hyatt sign to my right and made the move to stay there for the night.

I got into the Hyatt parking lot and looked in my visor mirror and cleaned up the coke residue from my nose although my eyes were as big as two melons and puffy from all the crying I was doing. But I didn't care, as long as I had my Platinum debit card it wasn't none of their business if I looked like Tina Turner after her fight with Ike in "What's Love Got to Do with it".

I got checked in and went up to my room and ordered several cocktails from room service. I commenced to continuing getting high off my supply and crying the night away.

My nerves were on edge and I was pacing back and forth in the room, I just couldn't keep still. I ordered movie after movie on pay per view, but I don't even know what in the world came on the TV, my mind was scattered.

All I was thinking about was what in the world was I going to do now. I'm alone, I am definitely not getting married to Benji's disgusting, cheating, lying ass and my girl, Jazz wasn't really even my girl. She betrayed me to the worst extent.

It's really strange but when I'm high, I am able to think very elaborate thoughts and it all seems to come together. But at the same time my thoughts keep bouncing to something else and then my original idea falls to pieces. I know that sounds crazy as hell, but what can I say, cocaine is a hell of a drug, from the immortal words of the late great Rick James.

I was thinking about what type of voicemail and text messages had filled up my cell phone by now. Surely, Benji was wondering what the hell was going on, since he was asleep when I left the house and oblivious to the series of events that took place with his cell phone.

My poor nose just couldn't take any more of the abuse that I was inflicting on it and I decided to call it quits. I could no longer breathe through my left nostril at this point, so the fat lady had sung for this binge episode.

As I was sitting there like a zombie in my panty and bra set, staring at the television with the hotel main menu glaring on the screen, evidently I had been watching absolutely nothing for Lord knows how long. My night had apparently turned into morning. The clock on the nightstand read 7:32am and I still hadn't been to sleep yet.

As my nose ran and drained and my high was coming down, I laid down in a fetal position and began to flick through the channels on the TV. I finally stopped changing the channels when I saw Bill Cosby on the screen. It was the episode of the Cosby show when the whole family was lip syncing to Ray Charles' "Night Time is The Right Time" song and Rudy was pretending to sing Margie Hendricks's part for their grandparent's anniversary. I envied that family so much and I realized that I was so far from ever having that type of life. So I just closed my eyes and tried to get some rest and hoped that when I awoke that everything that had happened was just a bad dream.

The hotel phone rang, blaring in my ear, it scared me to death. I sat straight up in the bed and attempted to get some clarity on where in the world I was. I looked at the big white door with the Do Not Disturb tag hanging over the knob to my right and the huge windows with the sun beaming in through the blinds to my left and then I remembered that I was at the Hyatt.  The clock on the nightstand glowed 12:15pm, it was check out time.  But I still didn't have anywhere to go, so I picked up the phone and called to the front desk and told them to charge another night to my card until I can get things sorted out.

Since I really had not had any real sleep, I laid back down and when I finally arose it was about 2:47pm.  Sleeping off a cocaine and Grey Goose hangover can seem like coming out of a slight coma.

I slowly stumbled to the bathroom and turned on the bright fluorescent lights and I was actually horrified with what I was looking at in the mirror. My hair was all over my head, I desperately needed to go to the salon and get my weave tightened up. (Even though I had naturally wavy hair, weave was easier to maintain...don't judge me!) My eyes had dark circles underneath; I could see my ribs and my pelvic bones sticking out from the top of my panties. I turned to the side and took a look at the butt that used to be there and it was still filled out a little but lacking the plumpness that it once used to have. I had mascara smeared around my eyes down to my chin. No wonder the guy from room service looked at me like a deer in headlights when I answered the door last night, I was a damn mess!

This cocaine thing was killing me and my life was in the same toilet that I was now sitting on. I had no energy and my stomach was hitting my backbone, I was so hungry. As I sat on the toilet with my face held in my hands, I suddenly had a huge feeling of depression that came over me. It was like no other feeling I could explain. I was thinking that my life had to be more this, more than what it had become. I had forgotten who I was in all this getting married, hustle-dope game life with Benji. I had really let go of all my goals and dreams just trying to keep up with him.

Just to let you in on something, you probably think Benji got me hooked on this coke stuff don't you? But he didn't. When Benji and I first got together this boy didn't even smoke weed or even touch alcohol, much less snort cocaine. He prided himself on making money. He said that he saw too many dudes slipping when they got high off their supply. Dudes would get robbed, set up, shot up and made horrible decisions when they hustled and did the product too. So at that time he said he would never touch the stuff.

The summer before I graduated from college I went to Atlanta for an internship, against Benji's wishes, but I had to go to complete my hours in order to graduate. When I left I basically had thoughts of staying in Atlanta to live and perhaps starting off fresh down in the A town. Although I knew that Benji was clearly upset with my decision to leave, I still somewhat felt that perhaps the time apart would be good for us to see if we really should be together anyways.

We had been together for about 5 years at that point. I was tired of the ups and downs of him going to jail, our houses getting broken into and the countless chicks calling our house. So I figured we needed that break. Better yet, I needed that break.

I was in Atlanta for about six months and I had heard rumors that Benji was involved with some girl from New York that he had driving for him as a mule back and forth from NC to NY. When I would speak to him about her, he would deny it of course and say she was just a driver and he wasn't even attracted to the girl. He would tell me that if I would just come back to NC then I wouldn't have to worry about what he was doing. The guilt trips and the paranoia lead me back to NC, even though I think I could have really made something great of myself in Atlanta.

When I got back, Benji had moved us to Charlotte and I noticed that he had lost a lot of weight.  His behavior, his complexion and his demeanor had really changed. Come to find out, the girl from New York introduced him to cocaine use, smoking weed and he had even turned into a Hennessey fanatic, all in a matter of six months.  All I could say is that bitch must have had a red cape hanging out of her va-j-j to make him do all that shit. Because in the five years with me, he had been squeaky clean as a whistle from any drugs or alcohol.

Oh yeah, by the way Miss New York became the first baby mama to enter into Benji's life.  Yes, the chick that was JUST the driver, so he proclaimed, happened to get knocked up by my man. I didn't even find out about the baby until she was six months old; that sneaky bastard somehow kept that a secret from me for the entire time the girl was pregnant. That was the start of my baby woes with Benji.

Benji was a new person when he was high. He seemed to have so much more character and he became even more humorous than he used to be. It was like he had an alter ego with all this confidence and for some reason I found that super sexy! I know I am kind of backwards to think a drugged up dude out of his mind is attractive, but that was what I saw.

One night we were at his boy Freeze's house for a party. That was the start of my new beginning on this road of drug disaster.

The party was packed and the music was bumping, we were all having a good time as usual. Freeze had a huge house way out of the city limits of Charlotte. He had these mysterious rooms that were in the back of the house that were off limits to certain guests.  Before I left to go to Atlanta, we would always go to Freeze's parties. But Benji and I never really cared about what went on in those rooms, so neither one of us ever went back there.  I figured there was a lot of real freaky shit and hard drugs going on back there and neither of us was into that... at that time.  But once I moved back from Atlanta, it was a different ball game!

As I was talking to one of the girls at the party I looked around to see if I saw Benji hanging around somewhere because I hadn't seen him for a good minute. I figured he was somewhere playing cards or cracking jokes with a crowd circled around him.  I looked over at Jazz who was all in some dudes face holding a drink in her hand; she was twisted and happy as hell to be out of the house and away from Norman for that night. I walked up to her and asked her if she had seen my man.  She pointed towards the back rooms.  I looked at her with a twisted face and said, "Are you sure you saw Benji go back there?"

Jazz said, "Yeah girl, I saw him going into the room on the left when I was coming from the bathroom back there." I just looked at her confused like this bitch is drunk, she don't know what in the hell she's talking about.  Benji never went back there.  So I had to see if what she said was true since I really didn't see him anywhere around.

I knew that the back area was restricted and on lock for most people. Not just anybody could get back there without some sort of pass code or secret handshake or something. So I asked the chick that I was talking to earlier if she knew how I could get back into that area.

She just looked at me, smiled and stroked my face real gently.  She said she would be happy to take me back there, but I had to be down for whatever because that area was for grown folks only. I admit she had me nervous as hell, but if it was all like that and my man was back there, then hell yeah, I had to go and see what was up. I gulped down my drink and followed her towards the back.

As we walked through the crowd she held my hand and rubbed her fingers across my palm as we got closer. I was feeling somewhat awkward and I was thinking that this girl was either extra friendly or a little lesbi-ish.

When we got to the back she talked to the big dude that was standing in the hallway and whispered something in his ear. He gave her a smirk and gave us the go ahead to enter into the room on the right. But I was thinking, Jazz had told me Benji was in the room on the left, so where was this chick taking me? But hey, beggars couldn't be choosy and I was along for the ride.

When the door swung opened, reggae music was pumping, a red light was illuminating the room and a huge cloud of smoke hit me in the face so hard, I know I caught an instant contact. There were several people sitting on the sofas and passing around blunt after blunt on these silver trays. It was crazy as hell. They were all zoned out of their minds and just rocking to the music.

We didn't stop there though, there was another door on the right of that room and we proceeded towards that one. My hand still in hers, every so often she would glance back at me and shoot me this sly smile. I just looked back at her with an uneasy grin and anticipation at the excitement of what I was about to see next.

When she opened the next door, it was a huge bathroom and she told me to sit down on the vanity bench that was in there. I sat down and was wondering why she had me in the bathroom. Then she reached under the cabinet and pulled out a baggie filled with this white powder and a bag of multi-colored pills. She sat it all in front of me on the vanity table.  I wasn't stupid, I knew that it was cocaine and ecstasy; I had seen it before but had never tried any of it.  Benji never really had all that stuff out in front of me like that.

I told her, "I don't do that shit honey.  I may smoke a little weed from time to time, but cocaine and pill popping, I'm too scared of that stuff. I don't want to be a crack head or nothing."

She smirked and replied, "Baby girl I told you that coming back here was for grown folks. Now if you want to be a real woman about yourself and get to your man, then this is the way you get on his level.  I promise you, I will go slow with you and teach you all about it.  It will be fun and your man will love you so much more.  You will feel him so much better than you have ever felt him before. Trust me pretty baby."

I was so nervous, but very curious at the same time. I knew Benji had changed since I had gone to Atlanta and we hadn't really been getting along as well anymore. Mainly, because a lot of the time, we just weren't connecting anymore. I loved my man to death and I didn't want some other chick to be able to get close to him just because I couldn't relate to him.

So as she gave me a cocaine 101 lesson and she answered all my questions, I felt that I was ready to try it out. First, I popped one of the blue pills with a dolphin on it that she said would kick in shortly. The first couple of snorts of the coke burned a little but it wasn't at all what I thought it would be. I always thought that it would have the feeling of when water goes up your nose like when you're in the pool, but it wasn't that bad. But the drain of the cocaine hitting the back of your throat and locking up your vocal cords is what is not too appealing. The taste is horrible but she said that is when you know you got some good product and that's when your high begins to kick in.

We sat in there for what seemed like hours and throughout the process I felt the need to smoke cigarettes and drink liquor just to keep the high of the coke leveled out. The drug requires a lot of companion habits. But overall I felt numb, like a high I had never felt before. I was alert and I felt as though I could accomplish anything. I became horny as a rabbit in heat though and that's when the next level came into play.

When I was all geeked up and feeling hot and heavy, the girl moved the vanity table out of the way and kneeled down in front of me. She then gently removed my shirt over my head and started kissing me lightly on my neck. Then she removed my bra and began sucking on my breasts ever so gently. I was thinking in my head, I am not gay, I don't do girls, but it felt so good that I just couldn't stop her. Then she looked me straight in the eyes and leaned in close and her lips gently caressed my lips and we began kissing; very passionate kissing, but gentle and soft. I was in another zone at that point. I unbuttoned her shirt and removed her bra and began rubbing her breasts as she unbuttoned my jeans. We both stood up and took off our pants all the while caressing and kissing each other.

She whispered in my ear and asked me if I was ready to see my man and honestly I had forgotten all about Benji during all of this. This woman had me so mesmerized by her affections that it had escaped me why I was back there in the first place. But I suppose that was part of her plan anyways.

We were both in our panties and she took me by the hand again and led me through the other door

across from the one we entered into. When we
entered that room it had a blue light shining and
there he was, my man Benji, sitting on the edge of
the bed. He was getting a blow job from some
random girl who was on her knees. I knew what I
was seeing and I probably shouldn't like it, but the
girl who led me in there squeezed my hand tighter
and kissed me on the cheek and said that it was
okay. So I just kept on following behind her like a
little puppy.

There were probably about 10 people in that
room, all naked, scattered around on sofas, beds and
in chairs, just getting it on in various groups and
positions. The girl that I was with walked over to
Benji while he was leaned back with his eyes closed,
enjoying the pleasures of his head job. She tapped
him on the shoulder and when he opened his eyes
and saw me he looked surprised but not startled.
She whispered something in his ear and he pushed

the girl that was on her knees to the side and told her to go.

He looked at me with such an enamored look and he motioned for me to come to him. He kissed me so fervently and then turned me around and laid me down on my back across the bed. He told me to relax and enjoy the ride. The girl straddled me and I was propped up on the pillows, she handed Benji the bag with the coke in it and he scooped it out and served me. She then moved down my body with light kisses and began performing oral sex on me.

As the night went on we engaged in a threesome with all of us being pleasured by one another. It was amazing but very strange to say the least. I was actually allowing another woman to be entered by my man and I didn't have any objections to it. I then realized what Benji loved about this drug, it made me feel so free and so open. I knew that I would have to keep it going if I wanted to be in his world and on his level from that point on.

That was just the beginning of many sex escapades and drug indulgences that Benji and I encountered over the next 10 years. I must admit when we were high, we always had a ball and he kept me laughing through it all. But the down slope was torture. Times seemed to be better when we were getting high than when we just tried to be sober and get along, all we did was argue. The days of clean and sober living were over for us.

As the years went by I had my ups and downs with the drugs. I would go real hard for months and feel like dying throughout the process. So then I would stop for a few months just to get some clarity especially when I so called trying to get back into acting. But Benji never stopped using and he would only entice me more to party with him in order to steer me away from what I wanted to do with my career. His drug use only got worse and all the while he kept having babies and not to mention the STD's he so generously passed off to me as well.

Yep, he burned me a few times and yep, my dumb ass stayed with him anyways. I suppose when you're a heavy cocaine user and you party all the time, you don't really care about anything but being in that moment and the high. So condom use is an afterthought in most situations.

In the last few years and after countless trips to the clinic, I grew weary of the sex parties and the Russian roulette we were playing with the diseases. Luckily, neither HIV nor Herpes ever popped up, thank the Lord!

Once we got engaged I thought all that extra wild stuff was behind us. I figured we could be a couple that could still get a little high now and then and just chill out together. We were grown now and it was time to handle our relationship differently.

But as you can see, Benji was still out in the streets, sticking his meat in any hole he could find. I guess there is no such thing as putting expectations on the actions of coke head.

So like I said earlier, he didn't get me on drugs, I got myself on drugs to be closer to him, or so I thought that's what I was doing. I can see now that I was just an insecure girl and I was so afraid of losing him that I was willing to dance with the devil just to be in his life. It was a stupid thing to do and I know I have to stop all this crap before it takes me over the edge. I mean before I started snorting coke, I had always been between a size 10 and 12. Through all these years my weight has fluctuated but now I have managed to dwindle down to a size 6 and it really wasn't a good look for me, my head is too big for this little body.

I pulled my little butt up from off the toilet and went over to my cell phone and decided to turn it on and check my messages. Just as I figured, my voicemail was inundated with messages as well as my text messages were filled to capacity. There were countless messages from Jazz and Tiana asking me what happened and to please just call them. Momma had left a couple of messages cussing me out and threatening me to call her before she has heart failure. Finally, Benji had to put his two cents in there and pleaded with me to call him and to just come home. Oh yeah, and that he loved me and was so worried about me being out in the streets alone.

I considered calling momma, but then I decided against it, I just didn't feel like explaining everything that happened right now. Plus, I was going to have to tell her that the wedding was off. I suppose I needed to mention that fact to Benji first so that he knew that it was finally over for good. So instead of dealing with any of that I had the bright idea to go over to the mall and get some new clothes. I could get a few items to at least last me a few days until I could get my clothes from the house or until I figured out my next move.

I got myself together, got dressed and drove over to Nordstrom's and shopped around for a couple of hours picking up a few tops, some jeans, undergarments and two pairs of Manolo's. I gave the over friendly salesperson at the register my debit card when she gladly gave me the healthy total of $2867.45. As I punched in my pin number and she was waiting for the approval code to come through she began taking the sensors off and bagging my items. My mind was somewhat drifting off and I was glancing around at some other shoes that were on display.

She said, "Excuse me Ms. Dubois, your card was declined. Are you sure you input the correct pin number?"

I said, "Oh I am sorry, I probably didn't, I am kind of out of it today. Let me try it again."

So she ran the card back through the register and I carefully paid attention to the numbers I punched in for my pin number and I anxiously waited for the approval code. I knew that we had more than enough funds in the account. I had just made a deposit 2 days ago of $8500 and that brought the balance in that account to $147,000.00. So I knew that in my moment of haste I had to have input the wrong pin number.

The saleswoman looked at me again and said, "Once again Ms. Dubois, it declined. Do you have another card?"

I was horrified and totally confused. I knew I didn't have any other cards with me and absolutely no cash. I began to panic internally, but I had to keep my cool on the outside.

I replied, "Umm , No hon, I didn't bring any others with me. I am not sure what's going on with that card, why don't you try and ring it through as credit instead, maybe something is going on with my pin number. This is very unusual and I apologize."

She ran it again as credit and that fucking machine came up declined even faster than the first two times. At that point I was distraught but I maintained a very calm and collective appearance to the saleslady. I took my card back and told her to please hold my items for me and I would be back after I get in touch with my bank and find out what was going on with the account. She nodded her head and said that she would be able to hold them until the end of the night.

I know that bitch was thinking that I either stole that card, was broke or that I was trying to run some scheme. I always figure that salespeople think that type of stuff when a black person's card gets declined, especially when I was purchasing that much stuff.  But hell, I really didn't give a damn what that girl thought, I needed to find out why my card wasn't working.

I got out to my car and called the 1-800 number on the back for Bank of America customer service and I went through the automated system to check my balance and when I entered in my card number it said invalid card.  I repeated the process about two more times and then I punched 0 to speak to a representative.

I asked the rep what was going on with my account and she told me that the card was reported lost/stolen earlier today by my husband and so they cancelled the card and were reissuing a new one to my home address within the next 5 to 7 business days.  She then told me that I could go into the branch and conduct business inside until my new card arrives.

I felt the blood rushing to my head and I became furious at the stunt that Benji was pulling. But I knew it was just a ploy so that I would come back home, but he wasn't going to get to me with that simple ass game. I drove across the street to the bank branch and went up to the teller to withdraw some money there.

When I gave the teller my id he pulled up my account and asked me what he could do for me. I told him that I needed to withdraw $5000, I figured that would last me for a few days at least until I could get a new card. He gave me this look like I was stupid and said, "I'm sorry ma'am, there are no funds in this account. It looks like a wire transfer was done today and all funds were transferred out of this account. Is this the only account that you have with us?"

I had to be in the Twilight Zone or on Candid Camera; I looked around for a camera crew to pop out and for people to start laughing and clapping because I had been Punk'd or something. But no one popped out. It was just me and that goofy ass looking teller staring at me.

I said, "No, I don't have another account here, I forgot that was done today by fiancé, thank you for your time." I grabbed my id off the counter and stormed out of the bank.

I sat in my car outside the bank and I tried to hold back the tears but they just started streaming from my eyes. I lit up a cigarette and picked up the phone to call Benji. As I was about to push the talk button, I closed the phone. I couldn't let him win this easy. He was being such an asshole right now and I couldn't let him get the best of me.

As I dumped the ashes off my cigarette, the sun caught the diamonds on my ring and the light blared into my eyes. I looked at my ring which once meant so much to me but now it was just a meaningless high priced rock.

I had no idea of where to turn, I had no money, I still looked like yesterday with the same clothes and drawers on. I couldn't call anyone because they would just try and talk me back into going home. So I drove back over to the Hyatt to get my thoughts together. When I put my room key into the door, the red light flickered. I stuck the card key back in and the red light flickered again and again and again. This day was getting worse and worse as it went on. There was no need to go to the front desk to see what the problem was; I already knew what was going on. My fucking card had been declined there too.

I started talking to myself and I said" Ayanna, don't give up; you can get through this girl. Think! Think! Think!"

Just then my phone rang with that" I'm Bossy"

ringtone again and it was getting on my last nerve

because of the irony of it all. Bossy??? Who? Surely

not me! It appears that I am not the boss of

anything right now; not my relationship, not my

bank account, not my friends, hell not even of my

clothes. I needed to change the ring to "Foolish" by

Ashanti, because that is more what I felt like.

I looked at the name figuring it was one of the

people I was running from but it was actually a call

from my cousin Terrance. At that moment I got a

great idea and I knew I could count on my best

friend, my cuzzo to help me out without ratting me

out to Benji.

## CHAPTER SEVEN

Fortunately, I had a full tank of gas, so after I told Terrance what had happened he agreed that I should boogie on up to Greensboro to stay with him while I get myself together. He also said that he knew a jeweler who I could pawn my engagement ring off to and get high dollars for it. Since I wasn't getting married I could at least have some dough to hold me over for a while.

He had finally moved out of my aunt's house into his own little house even though it was only down the street from her, he was at least out on his own. I really appreciated the relationship that he and his mom had, they were real tight. I suppose Terrance realized he had to leave his mama because within the last couple of years he settled down with a nice little country girl named Sharon and had a baby with her. They weren't married but they lived together and he took really good care of Sharon and his baby girl, Tera. I love and admire my cousin so much; he never needed to be all in the fast life like Benji or all the other boys from the neighborhood. It was good enough for him to just be cool with everyone and in turn everyone just respected and adored him. All in all he was just a real good dude. One thing about him, he never judged me over these years about being with Benji and he always has my back no matter what. I believe I trusted him more than my own mother, sister, or anyone else...he was really the only true person in my life.

So once I got to Greensboro and arrived at Terrance's little house, I went in and chatted with Sharon and played with the baby a little bit. I looked around at their home and saw that they had a real clean, comfortable house. It was a real simple 2 bedroom brick house with all the necessities and a decent size backyard. They had a black Labrador, called Frenchy that Terrance had since he was young and it seemed like they were happy with what they had. It wasn't elaborate but just enough for them. They didn't have all the drama and foolishness in their life that I had been accustomed to in mine. It made me think that money obviously doesn't equal happiness and they were proof that people can really be okay with simplicity.

Sharon had cooked some chicken, macaroni and cheese and collard greens, that girl could get down in the kitchen with her country self. I ate two plates of food because I was starving like a runaway slave. They had cleared out Tera's room for me and said that I could stay as long as I needed to get myself together, no rush.

After I was full and stuffed like a Thanksgiving turkey, I was in the living room talking to Sharon and then Terrance asked me if I was ready to go and see the jewelry dude. I had almost forgotten about that, but I knew I had to get some money quick and that was my only means at the time. I looked at my ring finger and rubbed my thumb over my precious stones and told him that I was ready to get it over with and to get on with my life.

Terrance said that we should take his pick-up truck instead of my BMW; we didn't want the jeweler guy to think I already had money because then he may try and stiff me on the value. So we got in his truck and rode over to the North side of town to the shop.

When we got outside the shop I told Terrance to handle it for me. I trusted him to get the best deal for it plus I didn't feel like negotiating at the time, I was mentally drained. I looked at my ring one last time, slid it off my finger, kissed it goodbye and handed it over to Terrance.

Terrance came back out about 20 minutes later and smiled at me with this this huge grin. He said, "Cuz, he hooked you up, baby girl. I told you that was my man.  He couldn't deny that ring...it was official."

I said, "For real, finally some good news for the day.  How much he give you?"

Terrance handed me the white envelope and said, "That's $25,000 G's in that there envelope cuz. You gonna be straight for a good minute."

I just looked at him and smiled so hard and then I glanced into the envelope and saw all those hundreds gathered together.  I am used to having money, but for some reason this $25,000.00 dollars seemed like it was my ticket to freedom or something.  It meant so much to me.  I could have never negotiated that much for that ring. He got over half price that Benji paid for the ring; which is great by pawn shop standards. I leaned over and gave my cousin the biggest hug ever.  He hugged me back and told me that everything was going to be alright.

I began to count out some money to give to him and he put his hand over mine and said, "Naw, baby girl, that there is yo' money. You need that money to get yo' life back together. You said you ain't wanna go back to Benji, so you gonna need all you can to get on yo' feet. I can't take yo' money. Me, Sharon and the baby is straight. You my family and I just want you to get yo'self together, that's most important. You ain't gonna pay us nuthin to stay wit us. Maybe what you can do is baby-sit Tera once in a while, so me and my gurl can hang out some night, that's the most I ask of ya'. That's my final word on that!"

I just sat there in his truck and started crying, as usual, but this time not for sadness or frustration, but for relief. I felt relieved and so grateful for him; it was like he was saving my life or something. It was so funny; the same person who introduced me to Benji was now rescuing me from him. I managed to squeak out a humble, "Thank you Terrance, thank you for everything. I love you cuz"

He replied, "Aw, that's nuthin cuz. Now stop all that weepin over there.  You messin up my pleather seat with all that tear water and I love you too."

We both just started laughing and headed back towards the house.  He asked me if I had brought anything from Charlotte and I told him that all I had with me… was me. I told him that I needed to get some clothes and underclothes before the ones I had on got up off me and walked away from being so dirty.

I said, "Does Four Season's mall have a Nordstrom's or Neiman Marcus yet?"

He chuckled, "Naw Yana, you only got $25 G's now. Girl, if you go to them high priced stores, you gonna be broke by tomorrow.  I got another place in mind to take you, I think you will do fine there and get some decent stuff for good prices."

"I ain't going to get no clothes from Wal-Mart Terrance, I can't fall off LIKE THAT", I complained.

He said, "Girl, ain't nobody taking yo' ass to Wal-Mart, even though that may be what you need to humble yo little ass a bit. But naw, we going to Marshall's. They got named brands at good prices. Sharon shops there all the time. She may not be as fancy as you, but she dresses well enough to look decent and to not to look throwed away."

I was thinking in my mind that I was in for a reality check, but I had to do what I had to do now. Thank God my car was paid for! At least I got something out of that no good bastard Benji, so I suppose I can do this bargain shop thing. What the hell, a new experience for me and after all I wasn't born with a silver spoon in my mouth. So let's go with the flow, above all things I am a survivor.

We got out of the truck and headed towards the doors of Marshall's and before we went in I reached in my purse and pulled out the baggy with

the remaining cocaine in it and I threw it in the trash

can outside the store.  That's my past and I was

heading towards my future.

## CHAPTER EIGHT

It had been a full month since I left Benji and the city of Charlotte behind. Throughout the past month, I have actually accomplished quite a bit. It's amazing what a person can do when sober and free to follow their hearts. I had called off the wedding first and foremost to everyone without any elaborate explanations. I had apologized to my wedding party and told them that I was so sorry for any inconvenience they encountered due to expenses or what have you. I told my bridesmaids to save the dresses and that perhaps one day I would still walk down the aisle.

I had a few conversations, or should I say arguments with Benji. I told him I wasn't coming back to him because he was no good for me. Of course, he lied about the Synthia girl AGAIN, what a shocker! He said she was crazy and she was lying about everything that she told me. Yeah right!! He told me that he had invested too much time and money in to me to let me walk away and to let someone else have me.  Basically, he was being very threatening, but I didn't let that bother me.  I would just laugh it off because his ridiculous threats didn't even faze me.  He kept telling me that he was going to have the last laugh and I am nothing without him, but a broke coke head.

Although, I do believe by the rage in his voice if he knew where I was , I know he would have choked me out or done something real messed up to me, short of killing me.  But he didn't know where I was. As far as he knew I was still in a hotel somewhere in Charlotte and that's how I wanted it to stay.

I had also convinced my mother and Tiana that I was still in Charlotte also.  Yes, I know, that's my family, but Benji is a very conniving person and would offer them the right amount to lead him directly to me and I couldn't take that chance.  I knew Terrance or Aunt Tammy would never snitch me out for any amount of money; that just wasn't their style.  Money didn't motivate Terrance to lose all of his soul like it did most people.  Although he thought Benji was okay as a person, he knew that I deserved better and he would never do anything to jeopardize my current progress.

I still haven't spoken with Jazz yet. From what my sister tells me, she said that Jazz told her that she didn't know what was going on between Benji and Synthia. But I didn't fully believe her and I just wasn't sure of any of them anymore.

Tiana had told me that after I left the house that day, she and Jazz both went back into the house and woke Benji up to try and find out what had happened.  Of course y'all know he had no clue, his trifling ass was asleep.  But she said they saw his cell phone lying in the floor in the hallway from where I had thrown it down and they gave it to him. When he turned it on, he saw the dialogue on his text messages and figured out what happened. He then told Tiana and Jazz a watered down version of what was actually said in the text messages and concluded with the girl Synthia had been lying to me.

He proceeded to have Jazz back his story up by telling Tiana how she introduced him and Synthia when he came by the store one day to give her a package to give to her man, Norman. He then told her that he asked Jazz if she knew of a housecleaning service that could come in and help ME out because he knew our new house was too big for me to try and manage the cleaning all by myself. Jazz turned him onto her co-worker Synthia since she had a side business cleaning homes. So supposedly that's when she introduced Benji and Synthia to each other, for that purpose and that purpose only.

He claimed the day that Synthia and her sister came to the house to clean was the same day he sent me out to the spa for a day of beauty. He wanted to surprise me when I came back home with the house being immaculately clean, because that's what I deserved. Yeah right! He's so fucking thoughtful! Tiana continued to explain that he told her that Synthia and her sister did more flirting with him and admiring the house than actually cleaning it. So he fired her on the spot. After that supposedly he didn't pay them and Synthia got mad and vowed to get even. So that's what she was doing with the text messaging back and forth to me. That's the bullshit he told my sister!

But the idiot left out the fact that I had seen the text messages on HIS phone not mine! So basically that story he told Tiana made absolutely no damn sense and he was just lying, as usual. I told Tiana, not to believe any of that shit he told her and that I had already talked to the girl on the phone after I saw the texts and I did believe her. Hell, I believe that low down nigga probably fucked her AND her sister in our house that day. Please, knowing Benji, I wouldn't doubt if he did it on my bed. But honestly, I really didn't even care anymore about any of that.

Tiana also told me that Jazz said that about a month after she introduced Syn to Benji, the girl quit her job at the Nine West store. Benji had probably started taking care of her. That's what he usually did with his bitches. Put them up somewhere and paid bills and shit. He had the means to do it, so I'm sure that's why Syn quit working at the store with Jazz. She never even mentioned to Jazz that she had ever come to my house to clean, so she just figured that Benji never called her to have her come out to the house. Well perhaps Jazz, didn't know, I don't know what or who to believe, so I will just give it some more time and leave all those people where they are, out of my life for right now.

Getting back to the good stuff, Terrance had managed to hook me up with a great acting gig up in Burlington, North Carolina, about 20 minutes outside of Greensboro, with this local independent film company. They were shooting an urban horror flick with a decent budget and they needed a leading lady vampire character. Since Terrance knew the director from high school, he had me go down and audition for the part. I got the role on the spot. I want to believe that I got the part on sheer talent and not because of my affiliation with Terrance. But hey, whatever the case, I got my little monkey toes in the door and I was going to give it all I had to give.

Everything is going pretty well for me now. I know it's going to be a journey, but I'm at least making positive strides towards my goals. I have even started putting back on some weight, working out for this role and eating Sharon's good cooking. With studying my lines for this part and staying focused on this project I haven't even thought about using drugs or even about all of Benji's silly threats to get me back. I have also found a little apartment downtown, that I can afford with my acting paycheck and with the remains of my engagement ring sale. I actually move in there within the next 2 weeks.

I am really proud of myself and although I do miss some of the things about my past lifestyle, I don't miss my past life, if that makes sense. I have gotten used to the idea of living and working like a normal person and not always having to look over my shoulder or stress over the possibility of the dangers of my life with Benji. I am finally doing things on my own and I am fortunate to be able to work in the field of my choice. It's a small production, but it's definitely a great start for me to get exposure and some acting credit under my belt.

I do miss having a live in man however. The late night rollover and the spooning in the bed while I fall asleep was something that I had just gotten accustomed to over the years. But I have to stay on track and not let my lustful thoughts lead me back to the devil. The after effects are not worth the few hours of pleasure. I have been thinking about maybe getting a little toy or something to keep me company. But I will have to wait until I get into my own place for that. I don't want my cousin to think I am getting freaky in his little baby's bed. That would just be dead wrong!

I was on my lunch break from the set and I decided to go over to the Starbucks across the street and get a Caramel Macchiato and a scone. Since I gave up the cocaine, I still needed a little jolt of energy from time to time and I could get that from whatever the drug was that Starbucks put into their coffee drinks. If you have ever had their coffee before, you know it ain't just caffeine that gets you hooked like Pookie to a crack pipe. I know there has to be something up in that stuff besides just a shot of espresso; they always have a line of people out the door. Morning, noon and night, but whatever it is, it is legal and it was working for me.

I was sitting at one of the tables near the window drinking my coffee and reading the Creative Loafing newspaper when this gorgeous man walked by the glass. I looked up at him and he smiled at me as he walked by approaching the door to the shop. His smile was electric and his features were mesmerizing. He was like Shemar Moore or Boris Kodjoe fine, except I could tell he had some Latino flavor mixed up in there too. I couldn't help but to stare, I didn't want to and I kept telling myself just read your damn paper and stop gawking at that man, but my eyes wouldn't listen.

He went to the counter and placed his order. I couldn't hear exactly what he was saying but all of the ladies behind the counter were blushing and fumbling over who was going to help him. He was a definite charmer. He seemed to have a lot of charisma.

He was about 6'0 ft. tall, light skinned, but with a tawny glow like he was kissed by the sun. It was the middle of November and the weather had a definite winter chill in the air. He wore a long, black wool trench coat and he had on some navy slacks, with a crisp light blue button up, tucked in and a tie with coordinating colors in it to set off the blue in his shirt. I also noticed that his black belt and Italian made black shoes matched each other perfectly with the same exact leather design. The brother was clean, to say the least. He had dark features, thick dark eyebrows, deep set dark eyes and the most beautiful head of neatly tapered curly black hair I had ever seen.  I suppose a lot of people would consider this to be a pretty brotha and that he was! But I wouldn't say pretty gay-like, but just a pretty man; kind of metro-sexual like. There is a difference between gay and metro-sexual, because he didn't look sweet. He just looked very well groomed and maintained.

He got his coffee from the counter and all the girls were still just standing there smiling and telling him to come back soon as he turned around to walk away.  I quickly caught myself and looked down into my paper like I had never even noticed that he was in there.  The next thing I noticed, I could feel someone standing next to me and when I looked up, low and behold it was Mr. Fine.   I tried to keep my cool and I looked up at him, trying not to appear stricken by his good looks and I gave him a very nonchalant stare.

He said, "Excuse me Miss, but do you mind if I join you? Or are you waiting on someone?" I didn't answer right away; I first looked around the shop to see if there were any more available seats. There were actually plenty of empty seats that he could have chosen to sit in.  So I quickly assessed that he was going to try and kick some game to me. So what the hell, I would listen to what he had to say.

I said, "No, I'm not waiting on anyone." Then I looked back down at my paper.  I don't know why I did that, I suppose he really did have me nervous and I was caught off guard so I didn't know what else to do at that moment.

So he repeats," Well do you mind if I sit here with you? I don't want to impose on you or anything."

As fine as this man was he could have imposed on me, sat on me, or done whatever he wanted to do to me. I was overtaken by his looks and his wonderful scent.  He smelled like he just walked out of a cologne page in a magazine.

I replied," Oh, yeah, you can sit down, if you want to."
He chuckled and said, "Well since you're so welcoming, how could I resist?"

He sat his drink down and sat down across from me.  He then took off his coat and I could even see that he had a good physique through his shirt. This man was going to have me falling out up in the Starbuck's.  He needed to leave that damn coat on.

He opened up the dialogue by introducing himself and stating that his name is Deleon Fernandez.  He said he was an outside insurance salesman for a major health insurance company and he was on an appointment in this area today.  He's originally from Queens, New York and he moved down to North Carolina years ago to attend school at the University of North Carolina-Chapel Hill on a football scholarship. He decided to stay down here to live after he graduated and realized his dreams of the NFL were over due to all his injuries. He said he was still in the process of getting his MBA, but has gotten so busy with work that he hasn't finished up on it yet.

He went on with his verbal resume to tell me he was single, thirty-something, with no children and he lived in a house in Greensboro out near the airport. I noticed he had an obvious NYC accent but there was a little hint of Espanola up in his dialect too. He told me that his mother was Black and his father was from the Dominican Republic. His father made sure that he was bilingual so that he would never be held back by the inability to communicate with a variety of people. I know that's right! I wish I knew another language too, like Vietnamese. So I could tell what those people who do my nails are talking about. They drive me crazy when they talk around people and then just smile in your face.

Anyways, he topped it off with the fact that he was a Christian and in love with the Lord. WOW!! I had never met one of those before. I mean a young, fine Christian dude like him. Back when I used to go to church as a child, I recall all the old folks shouting, running laps up and down the aisles and doing back flips over the pews. I don't remember any of them being young and handsome like Deleon. So this was very new to me to say the least. I asked him why he decided to come over and talk to me and he replied that when he saw me through the window I had an outer glow that captured his eye and he wanted to see what my inner quality was like.

Well, y'all know I was grinning from ear to ear; I have been approached by men plenty of times in my life that try and kick game, but never quite like this. He didn't try and say how fine he thought I was, or where's my man or any corny shit that brothers be hollering when they are trying to meet a female.

He openly talked about himself and then he listened to what I had to say about myself. I briefly gave him the outline about me. He seemed interested in the fact that I was pursuing an acting career; he thought that was courageous of me. It showed that I took risks and go for what I want in life. He compared that risk taking attitude to himself and his desire to succeed in life. Benji never really listened to me about stuff like this and the only things we ever had in common was getting high and having sex, now that I really think about it.

At this point I knew there was uniqueness about this man and it went far beyond his good looks. He had something in his spirit that was so positive that it flowed out onto the table. I wasn't sure if I was more intrigued by what he was saying or how he was saying it.  I do understand and I am well aware that since he worked as a salesperson they are known to have the gift of gab, and maybe that was part of his game and I just wasn't able to see through it yet.  I just knew that whatever it was, I had a genuine attraction to him and I wanted to make it my business to get to know Mr. Fernandez a bit more  to see if he was the real deal or not.

About an hour had gone by and we were having a great conversation until I looked down at my watch and realized I had to get back over to the set.  Deleon graciously asked if it would be alright if we kept in touch because he would like to get to know more about me.  Now y'all know I was more than ready to give this brother my number, I was actually going to offer it to him if he didn't ask me first.  So it was a relief that he beat me to the punch so that I didn't seem so desperate.  We both took out our cell phones and input each other's information.

We stood to our feet and he assisted me in putting my sweater coat on and he politely shook my hand and gave me a big friendly hug. I mean it was really a warm and friendly hug. Not like when most dudes hug on you and they try and get real close to your body and push their pelvises into you while trying to slip in a quick feel up and down your back. I didn't feel groped upon, it just felt good and secure.

We walked outside to the parking lot and he held my door open for me and told me that he would call me real soon. He gently closed my door and walked away.

This man was a dream; he was nice, polite, educated, handsome and employed. So that meant that there had to be something drastically wrong with him, no one could be that perfect.

When I got back to the set, I told one of the make-up artists about Deleon and how great he was. I couldn't stop thinking about him throughout the rest of the day. I was basically off focus and giddy reading through my lines. So the director cut it short for the day. He told everyone to take tomorrow off to get prepared for the fight scene that was happening this Friday. He was going to have to get the set ready for all the special effects and stunts.

Since my character is the leading vampire, she is somewhat of a slayer too. She has to do a couple of fight scenes to slay the evil vampires and the dregs of the underworld, but she doesn't harm innocent people. It's a very interesting film; I'm excited to be working on it. I am a little concerned about the fight scenes though because I only recently started working out again, but the director is real understanding and will provide stunt doubles if I need them.  But I'm at least going to try and handle the butt kicking myself first.

After the director dismissed us, I went directly back to Terrance's house.  I was so eager to tell him and Sharon all about this new guy that I met today. Terrance was still at work when I arrived at the house and Sharon was sitting at the table grading papers.  She was a kindergarten schoolteacher and I'm sure the nicest one in that school.  Any child would be lucky to have her for their introduction to the whole school experience.  She is just an all-around nice person; I guess that's how they raise them down in Smithfield NC, where she was from.

I sat down with her at the table and told her all about Deleon and she was so excited for me to have met such an apparently nice man.  However, she agreed that he might just be bipolar, schizophrenic, a sex maniac, a child molester or else he had a little pecker. Because all the good stuff I told her about him, was indeed, almost too good to be true. We just laughed about it. But she did add to his credit that if he was a Christian man, it really isn't that hard to believe that he is just highly favored and blessed. She then tried to assure me that there may not be anything majorly wrong with him at all and to just have faith.

Sharon and Terrance were not Holy Rollers, but they were good people and went to church pretty frequently. Sharon has a beautiful voice and she sings in the church choir and leads the children's bible study. She was a little more into it than Terrance was but I think she was making a positive impact on getting him more involved, which was real special to see.

In the past 15 years of my life, God and I haven't really been too close. I mean I believe in God and Jesus Christ, I just never made church and that kind of stuff part of my life as an adult. I suppose Benji and I just felt that God knew our hearts and after all we weren't terribly awful people. Well at least I wasn't terribly awful. There were many more people out in the world doing worse stuff than we did. So basically, we didn't really make time in our lives for religion. But it kind of got me thinking that maybe that was why our lives were so full of confusion and mess all the time. I suppose I always figured we were blessed because of all the great stuff that we had. But when I would talk to Sharon about that, she would tell me that the devil also blesses people who do his work in the world. That really scared me; I didn't want to have nice stuff as a result of being a worker of the devil. Maybe it was time to try God, hell, I had tried everything else, so I guess it wouldn't hurt.

## CHAPTER NINE

Today was my day off from the set. I had told Terrance and Sharon last night at dinner that I would keep Tera today, since I didn't have to go to work. Terrance still wasn't accepting any money from me, so I tried to do what I could around the house to do my part. I would try and make up for them not letting me pay them by buying Tera cute little Baby Phat and Osh Kosh toddler outfits from, guess where? My favorite new store... Marshall's. I knew that they wouldn't dare take the clothes off the baby's back just because I spent MY money; that would be downright mean and nasty.

It was about noon and I had just finished laying Tera down for her afternoon nap. So I began rehearsing some of my lines for tomorrow's fight scene. Just then my cell phone began to ring to the tune of "Me, Myself and I" by Beyoncé. As you can see, I took that damn "I'm Bossy" up off there; it no longer applied to me. As I took a look at the number I began to smile and I quickly flipped open the phone and pushed talk.

"Well Good afternoon Mr. Fernandez, how are you doing today?" I said, keeping cool, all the while wanting to jump out my skin because this man was calling me so soon. I was acting like a pimple faced teenage girl back in high school, it was so bizarre. I had not had this feeling in many years.

He replied, "I'm just great lovely lady, I had you on my mind and I was wondering what you are up to today?"

"Oh, well that's so nice that I made that great of an impression upon you that during your busy day you had little ole' me on your mind. I'm flattered." I said.

"HaHa, you are funny Ms. Ayanna. Of course you made a wonderful impression. You don't have to do much, just be yourself and you leave an unforgettable mark in a person's mind." He said.

I blushed and responded, "You have such a way with words. But as far as today, I'm actually off from the set, babysitting my little cousin today and going over my script for shooting tomorrow. How's your day going?"

"Well, it turns out that I only have one more appointment for the day in about a half an hour and then I am done. It's a pretty light day. So, since we are both somewhat free, can I break you away from your big movie star life for just a moment and take you to get a bite to eat?" He asked.

"That sounds nice, but I told you I have a 2 year old with me until about 4pm." I answered.

"Well, is the baby allergic to fresh air and restaurants? Of course the baby can come also. I love children; I have 8 of them myself." He laughed.

I giggled slightly because I knew he was just joking. But if he only knew that I just left a man with about that many damn kids in real life, then he would know that I didn't actually think it was that funny.

I said," Okay that's cool. Where do you want to go? I am not that picky, but I kind of just want a good salad today."

He said, "Well my next appointment is off West Wendover Ave. So would it be okay to go to a restaurant somewhere out there?"

I said," Sure, that would be fine. How about Ruby Tuesday's, is that cool with you?"

He agreed to the place and I told him that I would meet him there around 2:00pm. I immediately went to look for something cute to wear. I didn't want to look too overdone like I was trying too hard, but I didn't want to look like I didn't try at all either, so I had to get just the right thing together.

Since I have been in Greensboro, I had purchased a decent wardrobe, but my current collection was nowhere near what I had back at the house with Benji. However, I couldn't allow myself to dwell on material things because my peace of mind that I was gaining now was much more important than my designer clothes that I no longer had. I was working on humility these days and as long as I was blessed with some decent clothes on my back, that's what I should be grateful for. It was like I was in Life School or something. I was learning so much daily from Terrance and Sharon about the quality of life. My present surroundings were so far from the life I used to live with Benji and I was truly enjoying it!

I managed to put together something cute and presentable within the hour. I threw on some nicely fitting dark-washed boot cut Levi jeans, not too tight, not too loose and a cream colored v-neck chenille sweater with some pointy toe black stiletto boots. Even though I am blessed to be able to hook up an outfit on a budget, I sure do miss my Gucci bags, all of my Manola Blanik shoes and my assortment of designer fragrances, but once again I am working with what I got. All I could think about was that I hope this movie I'm working on is a smash, so I can move back up to the East Side like the Jefferson's. I began to laugh to myself at how shallow I was being, but hey a person can't change overnight.

I called Sharon on her cell and asked her if it was okay for me to take the baby out for lunch with my new friend. She said that was fine and to just get the extra car seat from out of the garage. So I woke the baby up and got her dressed in a cute pink outfit and bundled her up tight for the brisk autumn weather.

We arrived at Ruby Tuesday's before Deleon got there, so I got a table for the three of us. Tera was big enough to sit in a booster seat, so I had the hostess seat us in a booth near the window. I always liked to look out the window towards the parking lot, so that I was able to see who was coming in before they could see me. I suppose it was a touch of paranoia that was left over from having to always be on the lookout hanging out with Benji.

About 15 minutes had passed by and I had already ordered some French fries for Tera and I was sipping on a glass of sweet tea. Then low and behold, I looked out the restaurant window and I see a very clean, black Infiniti Q45 pull into the lot. It wasn't all hooked up with rims and sitting on big wheels, but it was just a nice classy looking car; it caught my attention. As I stared into the vehicle I noticed that it was my lunch date that was stepping out of the car.

He looked impeccable as he did yesterday when we met. As he stood up outside the car, he put on his black trench coat, but I was able to see that he was rocking a real nice shade of khaki green and cognac ensemble.

I turned my head as he walked through the door, so not to appear too anxious. I could see out of my peripheral vision that the hostess pointed over to my table and he was making his way over. When he arrived at the table, he bent down and greeted me with a great big hug and then he sat down. Tera was sitting on the inside of the booth on my side and he spoke to her saying, "Hey pretty baby, what's your name?"

I looked at Tera who was apparently blushing and shy by the greeting from Deleon. This man was so amazing that he even had a two year old baby weak in the knees.  I whispered in her ear and said, "Tell him your name baby girl."

She managed to babble out,"Nera", which really means Tera, but she can't pronounce "T's' that well yet.

He said," Well that's a beautiful name, for a beautiful baby."
She just looked at him with a blank stare and kept eating her fries. We both just chuckled and small talked about Tera for a few moments and then the waitress came back over to the table to get our orders.  We had been so engaged with conversation that we hadn't even looked over the menu, so we asked for her to give us a few more minutes.  As we looked through the menu, he asked me if I decided on what I was going to get.  I told him a Grilled Salmon Caesar salad but with ranch dressing instead of Caesar and in turn he said that he would have the Grilled Salmon Creole Entrée.

We were still talking about his day and what he planned to do for the evening and then the waitress came back over to get our orders. She looked to me to get mine first and as I was about to tell her but he interjected me and told her what I was having. I just looked at him and smiled. First of all he remembered exactly what I told him even about the dressing, no one had ever done that before. Not only did I find that considerate, I also thought that was very gentleman-like. I know that is probably a small thing but I guess I am just not used to that and I really liked it. Benji used to want me to order for him because he felt he was a king. That nigga even used to have me cut up his food and stir the sugar in his tea at the table. So this was a total new world of treatment for me.

While we waited for our food to come I wanted to know why this man was single, or IF he was really single at all. It was time to delve a little deeper. So

I asked him about his last relationship. He said that he hadn't really dated anyone seriously for several years and his last serious relationship ended on account of ignorance on his part. He began to look away from me and out the window as if he was reflecting on whatever messed up stuff he did to the girl. He had a very sorrowful look on his face and I could see the regret in his eyes.

He then looked back towards me and said," But you live and learn, right? God is good and just. So I try and use wisdom in my decisions now, so that I don't repeat the same mistakes. What about you? When was your last relationship?"

I didn't really know how to answer his question. I didn't want to lie, but I thought that it would sound really crazy if I told him the entire truth about the fact that I should be married right now. So I just said that I recently got out of a long term relationship a few months ago and I was hoping that he didn't want to delve too much further into my business.

He asked," So what happened?"

I began thinking of how I should tell him in an abbreviated way about the breakup. So I just told him that we grew apart and it was just best for the both of us to go our separate ways. I mentioned that I needed to get away from Charlotte to try and start fresh and that's why I moved back to Greensboro. He was satisfied with my response, so we left it at that.

I really wanted to know more about how he was so ignorant in his last relationship, just to be nosy. But I figured that I would just leave it alone since he let me off the hook about my situation.

The food came out and we ate and talked some more and then Tera started getting a bit fussy, so it was about time to pack things up. He paid for the check and we gave each other hugs and he walked Tera and me out to my car.He complimented me on my car and said that he would give me a call later.

It has now been about a month since I have been dating Deleon.  He is a kind and gentle man and he has really shown me a totally different side of what a real man is.

We do things like go out to eat, to the movies and we have even gone to a couple of plays and comedy shows.  We get along wonderfully and all of this happens without sex, which is a totally new experience for me. But Deleon was a totally different type of man to begin with.

The holidays were coming up and that's when I would really be able to tell how much he was into me.  Most dating couples usually spend some kind of time together during the holidays, so I would soon see if this could possibly be something more than

just a good friendship.

# CHAPTER TEN

Today is Thanksgiving Day and as the usual custom is; my family congregates at my Aunt Tammy's house for dinner on the holiday. So I knew that I was going to prepare myself to see all of the family that I have been avoiding so well for the past few months. However, it was cool because I was ready to face them now that I was doing well for myself and out on my own.

I invited Deleon to have dinner with my family. He excitedly accepted my invitation to come since he wasn't going to be able to make it back to New York to spend the holiday with his family this year due to his work schedule. I must admit I do have somewhat of an uneasy feeling about him meeting my family under the present circumstances. But I still want him to be with me on Thanksgiving, so I was just going to deal with whatever was going to happen. I mean with me running out on Benji so recently, canceling the wedding and basically not having too much of anything to do with mama or Tiana for the past few months, I knew it was going to be a slightly tense evening.

I had already talked to my Aunt Tammy about the situation. I was inviting Deleon, dealing with mama's attitude and then there was the slight possibility of Benji showing up, since he and I usually attended this dinner as a couple for the past 10 years or so. Tammy assured me everything was going to be cool because she wasn't going to have any foolishness or crazy shit popping off in her house with anyone... family or no family. So I knew she had my back regardless of whom or what popped up.

I told Deleon to meet me at my apartment and we would just ride over to Tammy's together. So I was getting myself together since he was going to be picking me up within the hour. I was really nervous about him meeting everyone. He had already met

Terrance, Sharon and the baby of course, but mama, my crazy ass sister, her man and my bad-ass nephew was a totally different ball game. I had already briefed him on the dysfunction of my family beforehand and asked him several times if he wanted to put himself through all of this on today. He just gave me that sweet smile that he would give out the side of his mouth and said that he thinks he could handle it. He said that I hadn't seen dysfunction until I met his crazy Dominican side of the family during holidays; it was like something off of a bad Latino sitcom.

I had also explained to him that although I hadn't heard from Benji in a few weeks, he was suspect to pop in because he knows this is where I would most likely be. I reassured him that my Aunt Tammy and Terrance wouldn't allow any nonsense from him if he did decide to show up though. At least that's what I was praying on. I really didn't want to see that fool or even have to subject Deleon to that nigga's drug crazed behavior. But just like usual, Deleon was as cool as a fan and said he wasn't worried about anything. He said he was just blessed to be able to spend the holiday with me and to meet my family.

I had just stepped out of the shower and the house phone rang. I grabbed my towel and wrapped it around my wet body and ran to the phone. The caller id read, Deleon Fernandez, 336-555-2899 and I smiled and picked the phone up off the base. Just to see his name on the caller id made me get butterflies. I still didn't know what it was about this man, but he just made me happy with his positive vibes. I mean it was a very different feeling because we hadn't even had sex at this point but I still felt a very real connection. It was a special feeling that I wanted to keep on having.

I pushed the talk button on the cordless phone and said," Hello Mr. Fernandez."

He said, "Good evening pretty lady, what's going on?"

I replied," Well, I just stepped out of the shower and I am about to get dressed. I should be ready in about 20 minutes."

He said," Okay that sounds perfect, I am about to leave my house now, so you should be finished perfecting perfection by the time I get there."

I chuckled," You are so crazy. Yes, I will be ready since you are just now leaving your place. So I will see you shortly."

He said," Okay darling. Do you need anything?"

I answered,"Um, no I think I'm good, just looking forward to seeing you. Drive safely."

He said, "I will. I'm looking forward to seeing you as well. Don't get too beautiful now. You may intimidate the turkey. Haa Haa."

I blushed as I said," You so corny! Later hon." He said," See ya later."

I sat the phone down on the bed and went back into the bathroom to finish drying off and getting myself together. I got all lotioned up with my Palmers Cocoa Butter and then slipped on my dark rinse boot cut stretch Seven jeans, size 9 and my black DKNY sweater. If you have noticed, I managed to get my weight back up to a good healthy size by working out and eating well lately. I went back into the bathroom to unwrap my hair. I was currently rocking a honey brown shoulder length straight weave that was very low maintenance.My hair took no time to get together at all just unwrap, brush and go, I was loving it.

I was in the mirror putting on my mascara when my cell phone started ringing. When I looked at the display, it read PRIVATE. I never liked to answer those types of calls, because someone was purposely trying to hide from me and didn't want me to know their identity. Which I think is so stupid. Why is someone going to call MY phone and not want to show who they are? Basically I had a good feeling it was sneaky ass Benji, so I didn't bother to answer it. I figured whoever it was could leave a message if it is was that important or unblock their little raggedy ass number if they wanted me to answer the phone.

So I went back into the bathroom and finished putting on my mascara and then the message indicator on the phone sounded off. It had already been 25 minutes since I last spoke to Deleon and I still had to package up the seafood salad and green beans that I made to take to Tammy's house. I don't like to keep people waiting on me when they have given me ample time to get ready, so I didn't bother to check that voicemail message at that moment.  Just as I was about to walk into the kitchen, my doorbell rang and I began to feel butterflies in my stomach, because I knew it was my Prince...Deleon, at least that's how I thought of him.

I looked out the peep hole and saw a distorted face that only showed a fraction of a man's face, but it was obvious that it was him on the other side of the door. I could see the fineness even with the distorted piece of his face showing. I adjusted my sweater and checked myself out in the mirror on the wall next to the door for any last minute fixes that may have needed correction and then I opened the door.

He looked very put together and quite handsome.  It seemed as though I was staring at him for hours before I invited him in.  I am somewhat still taken aback by him at times because he still seems too good to be true. But I'm going to hang in there until the fat lady sings. Like my mama said, if it ain't broke don't try and fix it.

He had on a really eye-catching brown and beige print Coogi sweater, dark washed loose fitting Coogi jeans, casual tan nubuck Timberland shoes and a brown Kenneth Cole lambskin leather jacket. I smiled and stepped to the side so he could come into the foyer area. He had his left hand behind his back when he walked through the door. He greeted me very warmly and gently by giving me a sweet peck on the cheek. Then he pulled his left hand around from behind him and he had a bouquet of white orchids in front of my face.

All I could do was to smile from ear to ear. I said, "Oh my God, you remembered from that day at Ruby Tuesday's. I can't believe you remembered. Thank you, this is so unexpected and sweet of you."

He replied," Of course I remembered. I wouldn't have asked you all those questions to just leave the information you gave me sitting on a shelf in the back of my mind. I usually do things for a purpose my dear."

I said," Well, once again, this was very thoughtful of you. Thank you. Please, have a seat in the living room while I put these in water, get the food together and finish getting ready. I will only be a minute." He walked in the opposite direction from where I was heading and I walked towards the kitchen with my orchids in hand.

He yelled out once he was approaching the living room and said," I know how a woman's minute can be. Should I have packed a lunch?"

I projected back to him from the kitchen, "Very funny! No, all I have to do is put on my shoes and wrap up this food, Mr. Comedian."

He replied," I'm just joking with you Ayana. Take your time, do you need any help?"

I said, "No thank you, I will be ready in a few."

I looked in the pantry for a vase, but I didn't have any in there. I don't know why I would think that I would have empty vases just lying around? I mean, no one had given me any flowers since I had moved in here, or in years for that matter, so I didn't have any vases on hand. But I did have a dill pickle jar that I had saved, so I filled that up with some water and put my orchids in that. I sat the pickle jar with my gorgeous flowers in it on my kitchen table. The flowers were absolutely beautiful but that pickle jar took away a lot of the effect. I made a mental note at that moment to get a pretty vase tomorrow for my flowers and possibly any other unexpected floral gifts that may come my way in the future.

I poured the pot of green beans with the turkey necks into a big Tupperware bowl and I put some aluminum foil over the glass casserole dish that I had the seafood salad in. I placed both containers in a large paper shopping bag and sat it by the front door.

I walked through the living room and told Deleon that I just had to put on my boots and grab my purse and then we would be out. He just smiled and shook his head as he flipped through the pages of the latest edition of the Essence magazine with those fine chocolate brothers on the cover that I had on my coffee table.

I walked back into my bedroom and took one last look in the mirror over my dresser. I then went and took my black Nine West boots from out of the closet and slipped those on. I walked into the bathroom and turned the light off, grabbed my cell phone from off the bed and put it in my purse.

I walked back out in the living room and put my hand on my hip and said to Deleon, that I was ready to go.  He closed the magazine and stood up and told me that I looked wonderful.  As we walked towards the door, I grabbed my keys off the key hook and told him that I would drive, since he had driven all the way over here. He picked up the bag with the food in it off the floor and we got in to my car.

On the drive over to my Aunt's house we talked about how each other's days went and how hungry we both were.  It's like on holidays you know you are going to get your grub on so you try and starve yourself the whole day to save room for all the food you anticipate eating later.  But in reality since you starve all day your stomach usually shrinks, so you get full a lot quicker. But black folks don't usually think like that, we just do what we do!

Since I was living on the North side of town off Cone Boulevard and Aunt Tammy lived off of

Vandalia Road, it was about a 20 minute drive, so we got a chance to chop it up on the ride over.

I again forewarned Deleon about the possibility of some slight foolishness with my family and gave him the opportunity to back out if he wanted to. But he just chuckled and placed his hand on my knee and told me that he was cool, he wasn't worried, and that he was really looking forward to it.

He always maintained such a calm and cool demeanor, I think that was part of what made him so attractive to me. His peacefulness was soothing and contagious. Whenever I was around him I would always find myself keeping a controlled attitude regardless of the situation. He is a very special man and I am very grateful to have him in my life whether it is for this moment or going forward into the future.

As we drove down Highway 29 I decided to give him a little more insight to my past relationship with Benji. I had previously told him slight bits and pieces of what had happened but I never really got into all the gruesome details of my former life. You know many people can take you with the bad but very few can handle your worst. So I wasn't going to take the chance and shoot myself in the foot before we even got walking to a good stride.

He already knew that I was engaged and I told him that I decided to call it quits before signing on the dotted line. He agreed that if you feel something is not right then don't do it. Deleon said that when you hear that little voice inside your head telling you what or what not to do, thats God and you better listen or in most cases suffer the consequences of disobedience.

I didn't even realize that I was listening to God at the time when I left Benji, I only figured I was just coming to my senses. I do thank God every day for giving me that word before I faced even worse consequences than I had already suffered over the past 15 years. It made me think of how many other times that I heard that little voice on the side of my head telling me something to do and I just ignored it; how different my life could have been a long time ago. Oh well, can't dwell on that now, I just have to keep moving forward. Trust me, now that little person inside my head and I are getting along quite well these days.

I figured it was time to mention to Deleon that there was a good chance that Benji may show up at Tammy's house tonight. I told him about Benji's drug addiction and that there would be no telling what type of condition he would be in if he did come tonight. At that moment I remembered about the phone call that I didn't answer earlier from that private number and the fact that I still hadn't checked the message. I knew that it was most likely Benji calling with some more begging or threatening, and I just didn't want to spoil my mood for the evening. Just hearing his voice disgusts me, I still find it hard to believe that I spent about 15 years with that crazy fool. But, you live and learn, right?

Deleon just looked over at me and told me to chill. He said no matter what condition Benji would be in if he decided to show up, everything would be just fine. But, he didn't know Benji like I knew Benji.

Benji always carried around a 9mm. in his glove compartment and when he was geeked up he wouldn't mind just blasting off. I don't think he ever hit anybody at least not when I was with him. But I did hear that one night when I didn't go with him to the club, he shot this dude that he grew up with in the foot because of some drug deal gone bad. He told me that he shot at him, but he didn't hit him. But they started calling the dude Two- Toe shortly after I heard about the incident. So that leads me to believe that Benji did do it. But he was a pathological liar, so why would I think that he would tell me the truth about that.

Needless to say, I did not want to get this really nice man shot on account of my disgruntled ex-fiancé. I would never be able to forgive myself for that.

Deleon then went on to tell me how very familiar he was with dealing with drugs and the tendencies of people who were using them. He reminded me that he grew up in the streets of Queens and then he said that he used to use once upon a time.

I said, "Huh? You used to use what?"

He replied, "I didn't know how to tell you and if I should tell you so soon, but it's here and no time better than the present. I used to be a crack addict. I was addicted for about 2 years when I was attending college. That's why it took me so long to graduate. But I can assure you that I have been clean for 12 years now. I understand that by telling you this that you may want to turn this car around and drop my butt back off at my car, but I felt that it was something you should know." He had a very disappointed look on his face, one that I never seen since the day I met him.

I just smiled at him and I put my right hand in his and I said, "Why would I want to do that? That would make me the biggest hypocrite in America. I appreciate your honesty and I thank you so much for sharing that with me. Before you told me that I was beginning to think that you were an android sent here from Mars or something, because you seemed flawless. To tell you the truth, I felt that I was not good enough to even be in your presence because you are a wonderful person and have been consistent in your ways since the day I met you"

He said, "You? You are the one who seems so perfect. I was so afraid to let you know about this.

I have told other women about my past before and they immediately got the thought in their heads that, once a crack head, always a crack head. I guess they thought I would pawn their TV or rummage in their purse for $20 bucks when they weren't looking or something like that. But as I said I have been clean for 12 years and I give all the glory to God for saving my life, that is why I put him first in all things because he gave me a second chance at life."

I felt so touched and at the same time compelled to tell this man who I had grown to admire so much, that the woman that he saw as perfect was only a few months clean of 10 year cocaine habit myself. I wanted to so much to know how he has stayed clean for so long and how he became the person that he is today, it just didn't seem possible. I began to tear up as I continued to drive, so much that I decided to pull off on the South Elm Eugene exit, which was at least 2 exits before where I should have gotten off. I had to tell him what was going on with me or else I was going to burst.

I pulled off into a gas station off the exit and parked the car. I looked into his eyes and reassured him that I still saw him for the man that I met him as. That no matter what he had gone through, I was proud and pleased to know the man he is today and that's all that mattered to me. I just hoped that after I told him what I needed to get off my chest that he would still look at me in the same way also.

As I began to talk, I couldn't hold back the tears from falling from my eyes. He touched my face and told me that it was okay and to take my time, he had an open ear for whatever it was that I needed to say.

I took a deep breath and told him that I had been on cocaine for the past several years and that although I haven't used since I had moved to

Greensboro, the thoughts do enter my head about going back to it. I told him that ever since I met him and started doing things for myself without all the negative drama from my former life with Benji, my focus was off of the drugs for the most part. I mentioned that I also didn't know how to tell him about all of this. I wasn't sure if I even should because anything could happen and I could go back to the coke bag any day.

He squeezed my hand tight and drew me close to him as he reached over the gearshift and hugged me so tightly. He told me that he would help me through it and that he understood more than I knew. The words that he told me were so warm and comforting. Then he said," I guess we have more in common than we thought, huh? Kind of like Bobby and Whitney!" Then we both laughed.

I asked him how he did it and if he thinks about it anymore. He told me that from time to time he does, he would be lying if he said that he didn't. Once a dependency for a drug is built up, the urge never leaves. He said that that crack had him gone. He wasn't himself and did things he never thought he would do. But with the strength he gets from the Lord and with N.A. (Narcotics Anonymous) that's what keeps him focused. But he added," It's an everyday battle for my life."

I asked him, "Do you think God will help me with this like he helped you? I am not as Godly as you. I don't know if He will give me that same type of help."

He said," Baby girl, God has a plan for you and He has already begun to work in your life. The fact that you made the decision to get out of your situation and have the willingness to do better, is nothing but God working in your life. Don't ever think that He is not here for you; you are just as much His child as me or anybody else. Trust in Him and he won't steer you wrong. Believe me, what you

see in me is a work in progress and He is not

through with me yet."

I said," Okay, what do I need to do to get to

where you are? I mean the peace, the calmness; I

mean you always seem so happy."

He replied," It's actually joy. It's joy in my

heart. God will direct your path. Just let Him do it.

Don't fight it. Look, if you really want to, I would

love for you to come and visit with me at my church

Sunday. No pressure but that's where I started.

Just being in the house of the Lord gave me some

direction. You can start with that and see where He

tells you to go from there. Pray because prayer is a

good tool to find your direction. Just pray from your

heart about what you want and soon you will see

things changing within you."

I said," Wow that seems so easy when you say it, but I'm sure it's much more to it than just going to church."

He said, "Of course it is, but you got to crawl before you walk. Just take things one day at a time. That's all you can do, don't put too much on yourself before it's time.

I said, "Thank you so much De. I would love to visit your church with you. That may be good for me; you never know what can happen. I feel so much better already, just to be able to share a little bit of what has been haunting me since I met you. I feel a huge weight lifted off me. "

He replied," Cool, well wipe those tears from that pretty face of yours. God don't like ugly! Haa Haa!! Just kidding with you sweetie. I'm here for you; I am a friend to the end, like Chucky. Whenever you need to talk, I'm here. Now let's go get some food, girl. I heard your stomach growling the whole time we been sitting here."

I just laughed as I took some tissue and pulled down the overhead mirror and wiped the running mascara from my eyes. I put the car in reverse and backed out of the gas station and headed towards Vandalia Road.

As we were pulling up in front of my Aunt Tammy's house, I saw that my mother's BMW X5 truck was parked in the driveway, my sister Tiana's Honda Accord was parked on the street and my sweetheart of a cousin, Terrance's pick up was next to mama's. So I took a deep breath in preparation for whatever was to come inside this house and I pulled my Beemer in front of Tiana's car and parked on the street as well.

I took one last look in my overhead mirror; I didn't want to look like Deleon had just beaten me up or something. I turned towards Deleon and said," You ready?"

He replied," Let's do this beautiful lady."

We walked up to the door and I rang the bell and Tiana answered the door. She had a smile on her face from ear to ear as she pushed opened the screen door and I stepped to the side to walk in. Deleon followed in behind me.

Tiana grabbed my neck and hugged me so tight and gave me a big fat kiss on the cheek. I could see she had a few tears welling up in her eyes about to drop. I hugged her back and then stepped back from her, so that I could introduce Deleon. At first I don't think she even noticed him, she was so happy to see me, it was like she had seen a ghost or something.

She said," Yana, where in the hell you been girl? You been missing forever and I been so worried about you. I mean the few little text messages back and forth let me know you were alive, but I am your sister, I need to talk to you big sis. Don't do us like that no more."

I just smiled back and said," I know Ti, I just had to get myself together, you know what's up. I'm sorry for not keeping in touch with you better than I did. You look good though; Cute sweater. Look Ti, I want you to meet my friend. This is Deleon. Deleon this is my little sister, well my younger sister, she ain't so little no more, Tiana."

He flashed a great big smile and held out his hand to shake hers. She just looked at him at first and then she looked at me. She gave him her hand, half-heartedly with a smirk on her face as she kept looking at me while she said, "Hello, nice to meet you Delee."

He corrected her," Nice to meet you too; But its Deleon."

She said, "Oh I'm sorry, I'm not too good with names. Where you from? Puerto Rico or something? Can I just call you De? I ain't gonna be able to member the Deleelee thing."

He just laughed as he let go of her palm and said, "De is fine, that's what most of my family calls me anyways. I am actually half Dominican and half black"

Tiana said, "Oh that's why you got that good hure, huh? I knew you was mixed with something. We got some Indian and stuff in our family too. My baby got that good hure like you from my daddy's side of the family. And..."

I had to interject," Okay, Ti, he doesn't need to go down our family tree right now. You a mess girl!"

I was so embarrassed. I meant to tell Deleon about the ghetto fabulousness of my sister on our way over to the house, but with all of our confessionals, it slipped my mind. But as usual he didn't seem fazed by her at all, he seemed somewhat amused.

So we continued to walk through the living room towards the kitchen and I could hear my mama's voice from the dining room. Tiana just kept blabbing as she lead the way, talking about the baby and how mama is mad at me, blah, blah, blah. I tuned her out as I was trying to gear myself up for my mama's encounter.

We finally made it into the kitchen and my Aunt Tammy was bent over the stove checking on the turkey in the oven. My mama was sitting down at the kitchen table smoking a cigarette. Sharon, Terrance's girlfriend was sitting at the table holding Tera on her lap and Tiana busted in first announcing," Guess who's here mama? Yana and her *friend*."

Mama just looked at me with a look that meant I am going to slap you silly when we get alone. It seemed like time was standing still for a moment as everyone stopped what they were doing and all eyes were on me and Deleon. I tried to break the chilling silence by saying "Hello and Happy Thanksgiving everyone."

Aunt Tammy pulled the turkey out the oven and sat it on the stove and said, "Hey baby girl, Happy Turkey Day to you too. Who is this fine drink of water you done brought up in my house?"

I said with a huge grin on my face," Well, this is my friend Deleon Fernandez everyone. Deleon, this is my Aunt Tammy, you already know Sharon and baby Tera and this is my mama, Evelyn."

In unison they all said hello to him, although my mama's hello was more of a grumble, but at least she did speak. I still hadn't really made total eye contact with her at this point; I wanted to save her for last.

My aunt Tammy walked over and first gave me a big huge hug and kiss on the cheek. Then she walked up to Deleon and he held out his hand and she said,"Uh-uh sugar, we a hugging family". Then she hugged him up too.  He kept a smile on his face the whole time as he spoke to everyone and greeted them all individually.

When he went to bend down to hug my mama, she leaned back and said," I'm sorry, I don't hug strange men.  My daughter has always had a tendency to bring in stray animals as a child, so I can't trust everything that she brings into the house. No offense or anything."

He stood back up and said to my mama," No offense taken Ms. Evelyn.  It's good to meet you in any case."

I was in shock; how could that woman be so rude to someone that I had invited as a guest?  She is unbelievable and I knew it was going to be some shit with her today. I just began to stare at her with such contentment and I felt my blood begin to boil as I was about to let her have it right there in the kitchen.

It must have been showing on my face that I was about to lose my cool because Tammy quickly said, "Why don't you take your friend into the great room Yana and introduce him to Tiana's man. Terrance is in there too. Go head y'all, dinner will be ready shortly."

I said, "Yes, I think I will go and do just that. C'mon Deleon, the air is a little thick in here anyways." I grabbed his hand and led him towards the great room.

On the way he stopped me and said, "Yana, don't let negativity of others, no matter who they are get into your spirit and spoil your day. I'm alright no matter what, so don't get upset with your family on account of their feelings towards me. I'm sure they have their reasons. I'm cool sweetie." He leaned down and gave me a peck on the lips.

I didn't know what to say, we had never done more than hold hands and kissed on the cheek prior to this. So his greater show of affection was an extreme surprise. Don't get me wrong, I liked it, I really liked it. His big full lips, pressed up against mine, even if only for a brief second, was enough to last me a good little while. It had been a good minute since I had some good total body lovin'. I admit I did feel a little tingle down in my jeans, which I thought was pretty pathetic since it was only a closed mouth peck. But hey, when someone does it for you, it doesn't take much from them to get you heated up. I looked back at him and said, "Thank you for understanding. You're right; I'm going to have a good day regardless, I'm glad you are here."

When we walked into the great room, Terrance and Chucky, Tiana's boyfriend, were in there playing

Madden on the small TV while the football game was showing on the big screen TV. Tiana's son, my nephew Austin, was in there too sitting on the floor playing with a toy in front of some older black man who was drinking a Michelob light.

I announced our presence by saying,"Hey fellas, Happy Thanksgiving. This is my friend, Deleon. Pause yourselves for a brief moment and say hello, please."

Terrance stopped playing the game and jumped up from the sofa and came over and dapped up Deleon and asked him if he wanted a drink or anything. Deleon said he was alright and then Chucky's trifling ass just waved and through his head up as to say hello. The older gentleman stood up and Deleon met him half way and they shook hands. I still didn't know who in the heck the man was but Deleon seemed to know him quite well.

As they shook hands, Deleon said, "Happy Thanksgiving Mr. Jackson. How have you been Sir? Looking sharp as always."

Mr. Jackson replied," Just fine young brother, I have been just fine for an old man. I recently lost my wife last year, so I am still working on getting through that."

Deleon said, "Oh, I am so sorry to hear that."

Mr. Jackson continued," Thank you son, it has been pretty tough, but I been standing strong. And then I saw Ms. Tammy at church a few Sunday's ago and she was kind enough to invite this old man over for a good meal. That's a fine woman in that there kitchen."

I walked over to both of the men and I said," Well good to meet you Mr. Jackson, I'm glad that you were able to join us for dinner. I am Tammy's niece, Ayana and I see you and Deleon have already met. How do you two know each other?"

Mr. Jackson just looked at Deleon with a real intent look and then he said," I will let this young man explain all the details. I'm old I can't always keep track of the in's and out's. But it's good meeting you pretty lady. You got a winner there De. Keep him on track Miss Lady." Then he went back to go sit down in the rocker across the room.

I just looked perplexed at Deleon and he smiled and told me that he would explain later. I thought to myself, what could be so top secret with this old man and Deleon? What could they possibly have in common? Oh well, as I began to let my mind wander, my nephew came running up and grabbed onto my leg, yelling out,"Yani, Yani!"

I lost track of what I was thinking about when I looked down at my precious nephew. I hadn't seen my boo in months and he had gotten so big. He was almost 2 now and just as handsome as ever. I'm glad he got his looks from our side of the family. I know this sounds ghetto, but thank God he was blessed with our family's grade of hair, because his daddy hair is nappy as hell. It rolls up and parts on its own; just peasy. I still don't understand WHY Tiana is with that nappy ass fool! Anyways!

I picked Austin up and gave him a big hug and kissed him all over his tummy. He just giggled and I introduced him to Deleon and he gave him some dap. It is amazing how the baby can barely get out sentences but he knows how to dap up folks and do the Rockaway, the Make it Rain and every other urban dance that's out right now. That's black folks for ya!

Deleon went and took a seat on the love seat and I took the baby over there behind him and sat down. I still had the rudeness of my mama in my head and I wanted so much to have a good day and to not deal with her. But I knew as soon as we sat down to the dinner table that it was going to be some more drama.  So I decided to get it out the way before dinner.  Terrance and Chucky went back to playing PlayStation and Mr. Jackson and Deleon were now engrossed in talking about the football game. So I figured now was as good of a time as any to talk to mama.  I put Austin down back on the floor to play with his toys and I headed toward the kitchen.

As I approached the kitchen I could hear the women talking about how fine Deleon was. I also heard mama throwing in her negative comments here and there.

I entered into the doorway and said," What were you saying mama? Did I hear you mention my friend?"

She replied," Yes you did.  I SAID what nerve you have to bring a nigga up in here when no less than 3 months ago you were getting married to Benji.  Did you forget how you just bailed out on him and our whole family with all this wedding shit that we had planned? And now you bring some banana boat looking nigga in here like you ain't did shit wrong. Benji has been worried sick bout you. Not to mention, you half ass told me what in the hell happened to even cause all this. I don't know where you been or even when you plan to get it together and get this wedding back on track."

I once again could feel my head getting light and my heart starting to race. Tammy motioned for Sharon and Tiana to follow her out the kitchen. Tammy stopped and whispered in my ear," Holla, if you need me sweetie. Talk to her, but just know I ain't having no shit in here today, hear me?"

I just nodded my head as they walked out of the room. I looked back at mama and said," First of all, you act like Benji is some upstanding nigga or something. That fool don't love me, he doesn't even love himself. He got ANOTHER girl pregnant mama!

Did your precious Benji tell you that? Huh? Did you want me to put up with another one of his cheating episodes and another kid that he had on me, huh mama?"

She said," He told me that some Spanish girl told you that to set him up. Yana, you know Benji is very admired in the city and women are always going to try and get to him by upsetting you. That man has been crying to me for months. He is so upset; he can't even get his bills straight without you. My truck payment was late this month because he was too distraught to remember to give me the money for it. Now you need to get your ass together and say goodbye to Juan Carlos in there and go back home to your man."

I just looked at her and shook my head, "That's what this is all about...money? You would rather ignore the fact that Benji is a disgusting coke head that sticks his penis into anything that moves than to see that I am happy now on my own. I don't want him or his money. But, if you are so worried about your bills getting paid then why don't you start fucking him too... if you haven't done it already."

She jumped up and slapped me across the face and said," Look here you uppity little bitch, don't you ever speak to me like that again! I am still your mother and you will respect me. You don't even know that foreign nigga in there and you think you doing something just cuz he looks good? So you just gonna throw away all those years with Benji for a roll in the sack with that Shemar Moore wannabe?"

I held my face where she had slapped me and I just looked at her really good for the first time in a long time for the kind of person she had become and I began to smile. I said," You know what mama, I'm not even going to try and talk to you about what kind of man is in that other room. You would never begin to understand. You have gotten so wrapped up in the life I am trying to leave, that you can't see anything but dollar signs and that is so sad. I like who I am becoming and I am doing things for myself for the first time in my life. I am very proud of that. I will always love you mama, but I am going to pray for you that you will see me for me, your daughter, and not for a direct link to Benji's bank account. I'm done talking about any more of this shit with you. Happy Thanksgiving Mama!"

I turned around and walked out of the kitchen feeling 10 feet tall. I had never really stood up to my mama like that and although I felt that I may have been a bit disrespectful, I only spoke the truth from my heart. I was a little hurt that my own mama would sell me out for the love of money. But I guess I created that monster, so now I had to deal with it.

I walked into the bathroom and looked at my face and it didn't look as bad as it felt. I put a cold rag on it so that it didn't whelp up. I made my mind up that it was going to be okay from here on since I got that episode out the way.  The worst was behind me now, right?

## CHAPTER ELEVEN

I went back into the great room and sat down with Deleon and the rest of the folks. Aunt Tammy had gone back into the kitchen, I assume to check out what had happened with my mama and me and to get the food prepared. She called Sharon in there with her to help her get the table ready. I grabbed Tera from her and I played with her on my lap while Deleon tickled her on her stomach and she laughed and squirmed around.

I couldn't help thinking about what it would be like to be holding my own baby in my lap with this man next to me as my child's father and my husband; like a real family, like the Cosby's maybe. I just wondered if after meeting my unruly family if Deleon even had thoughts close to what I was thinking about. Perhaps it was too soon for him or for me to be thinking about any of that right now. But I felt confident that in that small but meaningful kiss that he gave me earlier that I didn't scare him away quite yet.

Tammy started yelling," Dinner's ready black people! Come on and get it while it's hot!"

So we all started merging to get through the great room doorway and headed towards the dining room. The table was set so beautifully. Tammy had set out the good china this year. Most holidays she would just use the *nice* dishes, but she was trying to impress someone today. Not sure if it was for my guest or for old Mr. Jackson, or perhaps both.

I still hadn't had time to analyze the affiliation between Deleon and Mr. Jackson or even the relationship with Old Mr. Jackson and my aunt. I mean he looked just a touch older than Aunt Tammy but he was still holding it together pretty well.

He dressed well and had a nice clean haircut. He was a deep chocolate complexion with salt and pepper hair and a goatee. To be honest I hadn't really seen a man around my aunt in years, so maybe she was getting her groove back but in the opposite direction. I mean Stella got her groove back with the young dude and he turned out to be gay in real life. So I think Tammy had a better shot at keeping her groove with the old dude. He seemed nice enough and my aunt trusted him around her home, so he was cool with me. I would have to get the scoop from Terrance on his mama's love life later.

So we all formed a circle around the table stationed at each table setting. I made sure to stay as far away from mama as possible. I positioned myself next to Terrance on my right and Deleon on my left. Tammy sat at the left of Deleon, so we were well covered from my sister's loud mouth and my mama's hateful self. Mama was down on the other end from where I was. I couldn't even see her too well, which was fine with me; I wanted to enjoy my dinner.

Aunt Tammy asked who wanted to say the blessing and I just figured that Sharon or Terrance would do it as that had been the custom over the past few years. But to my surprise Deleon spoke up and said," I would like to do the honors if that's alright with everyone?"

All at once everyone looked down the table towards my mama to wait for her response. She would have been the only one to be so evil as to reject this man's offer to bless us. But she just rolled her eyes and said," Why everyone looking at me? It doesn't matter who says it, just say it already, damn!" Wasn't that nice, a great introduction to a Thanksgiving blessing; that's my mama.

Deleon just chuckled and asked for everyone to grab hands and to bow our heads and he proceeded to say the most heartfelt grace that I think I ever heard. He mentioned how thankful he was for life, companionship, food, family and friends and then he finished off with a hearty Amen and everyone chimed in with the Amen in unison. He squeezed my hand before letting go and whispered in my ear that he was very happy to be here with me and he thanked me for inviting him. Then we smiled at each other and took our seats.

Dinner was going along fine and the conversation was interesting to say the least. I just hoped that mama hadn't been drinking too much because that's when she would get really ignorant, but so far she just remained pretty quiet. Maybe she was thinking about some of what I told her earlier after she slapped the piss out of me. Picture that, I am grown as hell and this woman slapped me because I don't want to be with a dope head baby maker. How motherly and nurturing is that?

Most mamas would slap their daughter for wanting to be with someone like that. But once again that's MY mama and she gave me life, but I be damn if I let her take it away with her greed. I was letting my thoughts drift off to where I didn't want to be and Deleon must have noticed because he tapped me on the knee and said," You alright beautiful?"

"Beautiful? Aw she ain't all that! You gonna blow that girl head all up," said Chucky.

I just gave that fat bastard a dirty look across the table and said," You are one to talk, with your flat head. You just need to mind your business and keep stuffing your fat little face with food. Tiana, you better check your man."

Everyone started laughing and Tammy said," Don't y'all start acting rouge-ish now, we have company here tonight. We don't want to show them all our ghetto sides, now do we?"

I just shook my head and thought to myself, why everybody got to be all up in MY business; especially Chucky, with his sorry ass, no job having, no car having self; he had some nerve to talk about somebody with those rolls on the back of his neck looking like a pack of hot dogs. Once again, I was allowing these fools to get me out of my nice calm peaceful zone; come on back Yana, get it together, is what I told myself. So we resumed idle chit chat and I just hoped and prayed that no one, meaning Tiana or mama would bring up Benji or the wedding and maybe this night could end with no more drama.

Mama was still being surprisingly quiet and I started to have a feeling of uneasiness by the time the dessert was coming out. All I wanted to do was to enjoy my peach cobbler that my aunt made especially for me. She knew that I really didn't care for the traditional sweet potato pie that was served on Thanksgiving, so she would always hook me up with the cobbler.  But I couldn't help feeling that something just wasn't right. Mama was being way too cool for her to have just gone off on me.

Just then the doorbell rang and someone started tapping on the door with some type of object, because it didn't sound like a knock with a fist. Terrance got up from the table and went to go and answer the door.  I just glanced down at mama and for the first time all night she began to smile.  I knew that she was up to something.  Damn, my night just couldn't be complete without some bullshit from mama.  I could only guess who was on the other side of the door. But I just stayed in my seat and tried to remain cool while I was feeling myself getting anxious.  I didn't want to let mama see me sweat, so I just tapped my foot under the table to try and keep it together.

Terrance had been at the door for at least 5 minutes already and by now whomever it was needed to come in or they needed to leave. Since I didn't see anyone walking in, I assumed it was someone that needed to leave. Since I do know my cousin as well as I do, I knew that if it was Benji at the door, Terrance was going to try and get rid of him in order to save the family from the scene that he was liable to cause. I said to myself that I would give Terrance another 5 minutes and then I was going out there. If it was Benji, the only reason he was here was because of me, so I needed to handle it myself.

I was very nervous because if Terrance didn't come back soon, that meant that I would have to face the demon myself. I had been avoiding him for months. Now when I have the angel that had been uplifting me here by my side, all hell could break loose at any moment.

I kept thinking, little voice, please tell me what to do, but I couldn't hear it saying anything right now. Five minutes had passed and so I leaned over to Deleon and said that I would be right back. As I was getting up I looked at Aunt Tammy and then to the other end of the table at mama who was still smiling and enjoying her sweet potato pie like it was the best thing she ever had. Tiana said," Where you going Yana?"

I said," Mind ya business, nosy."

I walked out to the living room and I could feel my heart beating through my sweater, it was like I was walking in slow motion or something. It was just as I thought...the door was cracked and Terrance was half way in and half way out. I heard Benji's voice coming from the other side of the door. At this point his voice sent chills through me and I did not even want to look at him, but I knew I had to deal with this problem head on.

I pulled the door open and Terrance kind of got knocked off balance when I grabbed the door but he

caught himself.  I looked at Benji directly and said,"
What's going on? What are you doing here?"

Benji looked awful; I think the worst that I
have ever seen him in all the years I had been with
him.  He stood down on the bottom step of the porch
and he had a bottle of Moet in his hand. He was
wearing a black Coogi sweater, that was obviously
too big for him, even for wearing it normally
oversized as most guys do.  He had lost so much
weight in the last few months that I am sure that he
had been snorting coke for his breakfast, lunch and
dinner lately.  He also had on some nice black jeans
that were 2 sizes too big, hanging off him and some
black ostrich boots.  He did have a haircut and a
decent shave. But he looked tired with bags and dark
circles under his eyes and his lips were all dry and
cracked.

He gave me this big smile as he sniffled and
gazed at me with his eyes bulging out his head and

glazed over. He said," Hey Yana baby, girl I should beat yo' ass for makin me worry all this time. Is you crazy or sumthin' not answering my calls? Playtime is over now. You have proved whatever you had to prove! Ain't you sick of struggling yet? Don't you miss how daddy took care of you? "

I just sneered my lips at him and said," No Benji, I haven't missed your coke head ass! You were not invited here so why don't you just leave. I am doing just fine on my own, thank you."

He replied," Bitch, you got some nerve calling me a coke head, you sniff more coke than Tony Montana." Then he put his head down and looked back up smiling and said, " But baby I don't want to fight let me give this Moet to your mama since she is the one who called me and told me you were here. I wasn't going to come; I didn't think you would even be here this year since you had been hiding from everyone."

I said," I knew mama had something to do with this shit. Well Benji, I don't want you in my aunt's house with your high ass. Give my mama that damn champagne when y'all get back to Charlotte."

I took a step down closer to look him straight in his eyes and said," Understand this Benjimin. I am done with your ass. There is no more wedding, no more us, no more nothing. I don't love you anymore and I have my own life without you now. I don't think I can be any clearer than that. So even as high as you are, you should understand the words LEAVE AND GO HOME!!"

Benji just stood there smirking and pacing back and forth off and on the step. He looked like he didn't know how to respond.

Terrance said, "No offense man, you know you my dawg, but this is my fam and my mama's house and there ain't gonna be no shit here tonight, ya heard?"

Benji slobbered out," Fuck you nigga! You knew where my girl was all this time, didn't you? You a bitch ass nigga cuz when I called you the otha day you said you ain't seen this hoe. I knew you was lyin' and shit. But it's cool. You and your funky ass family can kiss my ass. It don't matter, cuz you know I got more money than all y'all niggas put together. So Yana you drown in your broke ass misery. I got me plenty of bitches at the crib wearing all your shit anyways. U will need me before I need you, you silly bitch! "

Then he threw the bottle of Moet at my head, but his aim was off. He missed me and it hit the door behind me and broke onto the ground. After that loud clash, the whole family was at the door within the next few seconds.

Tammy stepped outside and told Benji to leave her property before she called the police on his drunken ass. Then my mama slid past everyone and walked out onto the bottom of the porch with Benji and looked up at me to say," See how you have hurt this man Yana? What the hell are you doing? Stop being stupid and go home with him, you two belong together."

I was about to curse my mama out with all the might that I had, but Tammy tapped me on the shoulder and said," Evelyn shut the hell up with your gold-diggin' ass. Your daughter doesn't want that trifling nigga no more. Look what he just did. The nigga is crazy as hell! If you want to feel so sorry for him and want to baby-sit his doped up ass then you and him get the hell from out my yard and go somewhere else. I ain't having this shit here tonight. This silly nigga done already broke bottles and shit at my door. Get him the hell out of here unless you want him locked up tonight."

Everybody was just standing around waiting to see what Benji was going to do next and yelling out to him to just go home.

Then I could see Deleon in the background out the side of my eye and I was so disgusted that he had to see this horrific display from my people. Then I noticed my mama lean over and whisper into Benji's ear. Benji started walking back closer to the house spitting all over the sidewalk and he said, "Oh so you got a new nigga now, huh? That's what all this shit is about."

He looked directly at Deleon and said," Okay, so what's up nigga? You think you just gonna come and scoop my wife up from under me? Come on out here nigga!"

I said," No Deleon, don't listen to him; don't go out there to him. He is high and talking crazy. I ain't his damn wife"

Deleon said," It's cool Yana, I will talk to the brotha. He has something he wants to say to me."

My heart was pounding and my palms were literally sweating bullets. I just knew that Benji had his gun on him and that this could turn from bad to horrific within the next few seconds.

Benji looked at me and then back towards Deleon and said," So you went and got you a DeBarge looking nigga huh? Okay Yana, it's cool. Cuz I know this mothafucka don't have as much money as me and I know he don't lay It down like I do either! Do you? You ole' beige mothafucka!"

Deleon stepped out onto the step and replied," Look here my brotha; I can see you are real heated up right now and I can understand why. But this is not the time or the place for all this. This is a situation that Ayana and you need to handle between the two of you when the time is right. I am not trying to come in between that. But unfortunately she isn't willing to do that right now. So it is my concern as a friend to her that everything remains under control. So I'm sure when you have cooled off, you two can arrange a time for you both to sort things out."

Benji started laughing in an insane type of way and said," Is you for real nigga? Where you learn that shit at? Off the Cosby show? You came out here to *reason* with me, you think this is the Brady Bunch, asshole?"

Deleon responded and said," Nah man, I am just trying to bring a little peace to the situation as a neutral party. I don't want to see a brotha in jail on the holiday. I also don't want these good people to have their day ruined with unnecessary actions that will be regretted later."

Benji said, "Listen partna, Ayana is my woman and she always will be. Have your little fun for now with your United Nations peacekeeping looking ass. But just remember I taught that hoe everything she knows. She would be nothing without me, so trust me she will be back. She can't survive without me and she knows that. So I will let you borrow the silly bitch until she comes to her senses. Plus I look too damn good to go to jail tonight, so I will holla at you broke niggas later." He blew a kiss at me and licked his lips as he turned around to walk away. My mama walked away with him.

She is such a sellout; why couldn't she see how terrible of a man he was? Did she even hear how he talked to me in front of everyone? I was still a little shaky, sweat beading on my forehead, as I just stood there on the porch and watched them walk down the street to where he parked his car.

Everyone began to trickle back into the house and I stopped Deleon and grabbed him around his arm as he was stepping back through the door. I told him how much I appreciated what he did and that he didn't have to do that for me. But above everything, I couldn't believe that Benji really listened to him and left.

What I noticed most is that Deleon didn't curse or use any harsh language and he still got his point across better than anyone else did. Like I have been saying this man is something special and his positive aura even worked on a cokehead gone wild.

As we were stepping back into the house Terrance was headed back towards the door with the broom and dustpan to clean up the glass from the Moet bottle that Benji shattered on the door. I went to reach for the broom from Terrance's hand and he snatched it back from me and said," Go finish enjoying your evening with your guest. I got this little mama!"

Deleon had already walked ahead of me headed back to the dining room and I just looked Terrance directly in his eyes and said," Thank you isn't enough. I love you baby boy. You always got my back and I never will forget how you hold me down. You and Aunt Tammy look out for me more than my own mama."

Terrance noticed that I was about to have a meltdown right there in the doorway and he just grabbed me and said," Don't fall to pieces Yana. You know I'm always here for you, you my heart. Now get yo' booty in that dining room and finish your cobbler. It's over for now. Don't let Benji mess up the rest of yo' night, hold it together lil' sis."

I sucked it up and looked him in the eye like a soldier would to his commander and said," Yes sir, going to the dining room now, sir. Love you baby, always and forever, you my nigga if you don't get no bigger, sir!" We both laughed and hit me on the leg with the broom.

So once I got back into the dining room I was emotionally drained, but I didn't want to spoil the rest of the evening for Deleon and for my family. So I helped Aunt Tammy clear off the table after dessert was completed and then I heard Tiana yell out from the great room that it was time for the Old School music game.

When I was putting the dishes into the dishwasher Aunt Tammy reminded me that she told me she wasn't going to have no shit at her house. She said that Benji had about 2 more seconds and if he didn't get his narrow disrespectful ass off her porch she was going to pop a cap in him before she called the police. We both just started laughing and she pulled me close to her and gave me a big hug. She said," Your mama loves you Yana, she just ain't in her right mind right now.  She will get it together

soon.  You should have never spoiled the bitch by

paying for all her stuff, you know that!"

I nodded my head and said," I know, it's my

own fault.  I turned my mama out with money!

Damn!"

At that moment Terrance came back into the

kitchen with a bag full of glass from the bottle he

cleaned from the doorway and he just looked at me

and said," You holding it together little mama?"

I replied, "Yeah I'm good.  Now let's go and

beat some butt cuz in Old School music game like we

always do."

Tammy said, "Yeah right, y'all not gonna win

tonight.  I got my old school buddy, Mr. Jackson,

here tonight as my partner, we gonna stomp y'all

youngsters out!" We all laughed and walked into the

great room.

Tiana had already got everyone grouped off to play the game. She had paired Deleon and Mr. Jackson together and she was with her stupid boyfriend Chucky, who never knew any of the songs anyways. Then when all three of us came into the room, she pointed to Tammy to go stand next to Sharon and then me and Terrance were partners as usual. Both the babies were on the floor playing. Mama wasn't back in the house yet, but it didn't matter she was no good at this game anyways; she could never remember the names of the songs.

The object of the game was for each group to hum or sing a small piece of a song. Then the first group able to name the complete title of the song and sing at least one complete verse of the song correctly would get a point. But the songs had to be from the 50's through the 90's, no real new stuff.

Like I said earlier Terrance and I always won, because we both loved music so much and stayed up with all types of music over the years. He is the only person who ever understood my sincere passion for music, because he had the passion himself. He had a huge collection of cd's and he still even had actual vinyl albums from when he used to deejay back in the day.

Aunt Tammy decided to let the groups that Tiana put together stay as they were. She said she was confident in her skills, but truth is everyone knew that cuz and me were gonna beat their socks off.

Everyone had a ball, Terrance and I won the game as usual; I was really surprised with how much Deleon and even old Mr. Jackson knew. I was impressed. Deleon seemed to have enjoyed himself.

During the game mama came slithering back in. She sat in the corner and played with Austin and Tera while she sipped on her Gin and tonic.

I didn't say anything else to mama while she was in there; we were having fun in spite of her attempts to sabotage me. Once the game was over, both of the babies were asleep and I was pretty tired myself. I knew that Deleon had to do some work tomorrow, so I asked him if he was ready to motivate and he politely said whenever I was ready was fine with him.

I went into the kitchen where Tammy was and told her that I would get my dishes from the beans and seafood salad later. She said, "You and your friend better take some plate's home with y'all. I can't eat all this food. I have a figure to watch or maybe that someone else will be watching. Ya know what I mean?" And we laughed.

So I packed up a plate for myself and Deleon to take home and we kissed the babies while they slept, gave out the goodbye hugs and wished everyone well as we headed for the door. Right

233

before I got to the door, Tiana came walking over to me and said," I know mama ain't right for how she acting Yana. But I ain't her and please keep in touch with me. I miss you sis. Where you staying at anyways?"

I gave her a hug and said that I would keep in touch. But at this point I didn't trust her intentions any more than my mamas. I wasn't about to tell her where I was living.

I looked around once we got outside to see if I saw any traces of crazy ass Benji, but I didn't and we proceeded towards my car. Deleon took the take home plates from out of my hand and walked me to the driver door and held it opened until I got in. He's a true gentleman, and he always did that anytime we went out together.

On the ride home I knew there was a lot to say to each other but it was like we were saying it silently. He held my right hand and rubbed it ever so gently the entire way back to my house.  And every now and then he would lean over and kiss me on the cheek.  We said a whole lot without ever saying anything.

When I pulled up into my parking lot we sat in the car for a moment and we looked at each other. He caressed the side of my face and he cupped my chin in his big strong hand.  I grabbed hold to his hand on my chin and I began to kiss his wrist very gently.  Then he slid his face closer to mine and kissed me on the forehead and then worked his way down to my eyelid and then the bridge of my nose and he stopped at my lips.  He pressed those luscious lips into mine for the second time tonight but this time he opened his lip, which forced me to open mine, and then we were officially kissing each other.  He is a great kisser, just as I thought he would be. We kissed each other very intently and gently.

I had been kissing the same man for so many years that this was new for me. Kissing Benji was never any big deal and whenever we would start to kiss, 10 seconds later we were naked and bumping and grinding. It was like the kissing with Benji was just a quick way to get to my panties from the very beginning; there was never any passion or consideration, like it was right now with Deleon.

It was as though he was talking to me with his tongue. And his tongue was telling me not to dwell on the events of tonight and that all will be okay. I even heard his voice replaying in my head to have faith in the Lord and everything will be alright.

I opened my eyes and looked at Deleon who was now talking to me about trusting in God and that no matter what, everything will be alright. I blinked my eyes and touched my lips and then I realized my crazy ass must have blanked out or I else I had totally lost my mind. I mean I felt funny all of a sudden. I thought to myself, did we even kiss at all or did I imagine that entire episode? What was going on?

He stopped talking and said," Ayana, are you okay sweetie? It's like you just saw a ghost or something."

I said, "Umm, no, I'm cool. I guess I was just daydreaming. I'm sorry; I am just a little tired from everything that happened today. I just need to get some rest, that's all."

He said," Yeah, you had a rough day, let me help you get this stuff into the house and then I will take off and let you get some rest sweetie."

We walked into my apartment and went into the kitchen and he sat the food on the counter. I just put my hands over my face and started to cry. I had been holding in all these emotions from this evening and they forced themselves out all at once, right in front of Deleon. My tears don't have any shame. He came over to me and wrapped his strong arms around me and rubbed my back. We just stood and rocked back and forth for a while.

I asked him if he didn't mind staying with me until I fell asleep. I told him that I didn't want to be alone right now. He said," No problem, I told you I am here if you need me."

I said," As soon as I start snoring, which unfortunately I do from time to time, you can leave me and just lock my bottom lock. I would appreciate this as long as it's not going to interfere with you working tomorrow."

He said, "Ayana, let me tell you what I really have going on tomorrow? No more secrets."

I said nervously, "Secrets? You don't have something to do for work tomorrow?"

He said, "Well no, I told you that before because I hadn't told you about my addiction yet? But truth is, ever since I have been clean, on the day after Thanksgiving, my N.A. group sponsors a brunch for the people of Joshua House. Joshua House is a safe haven for men in transition from getting off the streets and off drugs. Many of them may be months or years clean and sober, but some may be days or hours clean. So there is a wide array of people that show up. But we feed them until the last person comes in no matter what their situation is."

I said, "Wow, that's great, but why wouldn't you have been able to tell me that? I would love to help out too."

He said, "That's what I was afraid of before. Since the members of NA sponsor the brunch, I was too leery of you asking me what my affiliation may have been with the NA group. Then I would have been forced to tell you about my addiction and then risk possibly losing you before I even have you. So now that you know about all that, then I would love for you to come and help out."

I blushed and replied," I have a question for you. What is going through your mind about me, after everything that went on tonight? I mean you've seen what is in my gene pool; you've seen Benji and heard about my drug issue. Now I'm thinking that it's probably gonna scare you off."

He smiled and replied, "Hey now, I am not judgmental. I think you are a beautiful woman inside and out Ms. Dubois." He said, "Any man would be blessed to have you. If it is in His will then perhaps I may be that man. All of what I saw today only makes you the person you are today. I can see that you are a wonderful work in progress with so much potential. But you have to be able to see that too and not let what you can't control defeat you. But I don't want to get too deep on you right now."

How ironic that I was thinking the same thing earlier tonight at my aunt's house about him and I. That if it is meant for us to be that we will be.

But after the fiasco that took place, I just knew that he was going to jump in his car once we got back to my house and I would never hear from him again. But I was wrong and he didn't run from me. He was still here and holding onto me with such compassion and caring that he made me feel very safe and secure in his arms and in his presence.

After I calmed down a bit he asked me if I was ready to lie down. I told him that I was and I grabbed his hand and led him towards my bedroom. He stopped at the entrance of my bedroom door. He told me to go and get myself together for bed and to call him in when I was ready for him to come and sit down next to me. I turned around and looked at him with a confused look. Sit down?

I was thinking that from the kiss in the car and my invitation for him to stay with me and the emotions that were floating through the air between us, that he would want to undress me himself. So he once again threw me for a loop. This dude was full of surprises to say the least.

So I turned and walked into my room and closed the door and proceeded to take my clothes off. I then put on my bathrobe and walked back out into the living room and asked him why he didn't want to follow me into the bedroom.

He said that he told me that he would stay with me until I went to sleep but he had already gotten himself past the point of his limitations when we were in the car. He had to get his thoughts together before he came into the room with me if he was to keep himself together. All I could think of is that We did kiss in the car! I am not crazy. But why did I black out for a minute? Very strange!

I was at least glad to hear that he was attracted to me, I guess. But I didn't understand why he didn't want to get busy. It had been over a month since we had been dating and I wanted this man and I wanted him bad. How long do people wait these days to get it on?

However, I guess this had something to do with what he had going on with God. But once again I don't understand what the big deal is. I know a lot of folks that go to church that still get their freak on all the time. They consider themselves to be just as spiritual as the next.

Now I am thinking that he may just be making excuses for not wanting to have sex with me. Maybe something was really wrong with his "little man" like Sharon and I had discussed when I first met him. Everything else seemed so perfect about him, so the sex part of him was probably whack. That's what it had to be.

I was standing there looking at him sitting on my sofa as if he was a big piece of caramel candy and I walked over and sat down next to him. I looked into his eyes and I could see a stress line going across his forehead. He was obviously troubled by all of this. I thought to myself if this man is going through all of this emotional turmoil over getting a little booty then I won't put him through the anymore stress.

I said," Deleon, I don't want to get you into anything that you don't feel comfortable with, so if you don't want to stay then I will be alright. You can leave if you need to go."

He said," No, Yana, I do want to stay. BELIEVE ME, I really want to stay, I just have not been put into this type of situation in a long, long time. It may be something that you don't understand, but if I lay with you naturally I am going to want to be with you. It's been SO long for me and I am extremely attracted to you. So it will be ultimate torture to lie in a bed next to you and not want to get physical. I am just not sure that I am strong enough for all that at this moment."

I was listening to him and becoming more and more interested in why he felt the way he did about going against what he had made a commitment to God not to do. He explained to me that God has saved his life and given him another chance. The small things in this world that He asks of him to do are nothing in comparison to what God has done for him.

As the night went on, I asked more and more questions about God and Christianity. He eagerly told me more and more answers about why he felt so strongly and what being a child of Christ meant to Him.

He explained that although he still makes many mistakes the Lord is still working on him, and he placed his hand on mine. He looked at me with those beautiful brown eyes and told me that the flesh is very weak and because he is still a fleshly being, he tries not to put himself in compromising situations because once that door opens for him, it's off to the races.

He said, "I am having a really difficult time right now, for real, because I really want to do what my body wants to do and say bump what my mind and spirit are saying."

I said," Deleon, you have more strength from the inside out and I don't want to pull you away from anything that you have going on. I am not going to be the serpent in your garden. Stay focused, that's what makes you so incredible and different from most other men."

I mean to be as fine as he is, walking around with women wanting to throwing their panties in his face just trying to be with him. He is able to refuse because God has a plan for him, as he says. Incredible!

As I sat there and we talked the night away, I forgot all about wanting to have sex with him. Well not totally forgot, but I cooled it off and the urge had somewhat left me. He has an inner spirit of some kind of magic in him and he allows it to pour out of him like no one else I have ever known.

I wanted him to keep that thing that he had going on with God. That's what makes him different and so very special. He is walking and talking a unique type of way and I didn't want to take that away and have him regretting anything. We had been talking so much and I had been learning so much about him and the Word, that I wasn't even worried about any of the things that had happened earlier tonight.

It was now 4:15am and I agreed to go and work with him at the N.A. event later today. So I thought he should get home and get some real rest.

He agreed and gave me a huge hug and another light peck on the lips. He told me thank you for understanding all of this. I walked him to the door. As I was watching him walk down the walkway, I glanced over and tried to focus my eyes through the darkness of the morning to the spot in the parking lot where my car was parked.  But as I kept blinking and trying to focus, I realized that my BMW was no longer there.  My mind immediately started racing through the series of events that occurred before we arrived at my apartment.  I started placing move by move to make sure that I had parked my car where I thought I did.  But before I could finish my train of thought Deleon came walking back up the walkway and said, "Hon, where is your car?"

A huge pit filled in the bottom of my stomach and I felt empty. It was now confirmed by his question, that my car had been stolen.  I stepped out into the cool air, not really phased by it at this time and I pulled the strings on my robe a little tighter and walked down the walkway with Deleon to look at the spot where my car once sat.

I looked all around the parking lot and then I asked him," Didn't I park right here?"

He said, "Yes, you did. It looks like unfortunately someone got you. Aw man, I'm hating this happened to you sweetheart. Do you have a tracking device on your car?"

I replied," I unhooked it. I didn't want Benji to be able to locate me when I left him. Let me call my insurance people. This is so crazy and on Thanksgiving night of all times. Damn!"

Deleon put his arm around me and we walked back up the walkway into my apartment. I am not even going to lie; I wanted to burst out into tears. But I didn't want Deleon to see me bawling like a baby over such a material object. So I held it in and I only let a few tears trickle down.

I walked into my bedroom to get my cell phone; I have my insurance company information in my memo pad section of my phone. When I picked up the phone I noticed there was 1 missed call from a PRIVATE number at 3:45am. So I knew it must be that damn Benji again. The message indicator was still on from earlier in the night because I didn't check the message, so I pushed the envelope button on the phone and called into my voicemail.

The first message was from Benji at about 4:40pm Thanksgiving Day saying that he missed me and that he hopes I find it in my heart to come home today, so that he has something to be thankful for. Blah, blah, blah...I deleted that message before he even finished talking. The second message was at 3:46am from Benji again. He was stating that since I wanted to be so independent and didn't need him for nothing then I don't need that BMW 750Li that he bought for me with HIS money. He said since I am with Rico Suave now then see if he can get me riding again, because he isn't going to have no other dude up in the ride he bought, trying to kick it with me. He said that I could have all my stuff back if I just come to my senses and get my ass back home where I belong.

I hit the END button on the phone and I sat on the bed and the tears came flowing down. That car was all that I had managed to salvage out of that stupid ass relationship and now that bastard took that from me too. He was a cold heartless dog in my eyes. At that moment I hated the ground that he walked on. If I had a gun and he was in front of my face at that moment, I would have shot him straight through his heart. In my opinion he didn't have one that pumped blood anyways; more like ice and of course, cocaine.

I guess Deleon heard my sniffling since my apartment wasn't that big and he came to my bedroom doorway. He said," Yana, it's going to be alright sweetie. Your insurance company will take care of everything for you. You had full coverage didn't you?"

I just looked up at him and replied," Yes, but it wasn't actually stolen. It was repossessed."

He gave me a confused look and said," How? Isn't your car paid for?"

I replied," Yes and the person who technically paid for took it back. That asshole! Excuse my language."

Deleon said," Benji took your car? How do you know?"

I said," The bastard left me a voicemail message telling me what he did. He has managed to take bit by bit of everything from me. Every time I try and put a piece together he manages to knock me down a little more. I sometimes think that it will just be easier to do what he wants and go back and just deal with him."

Deleon said," Well you know that I don't like that option of you going back. But let me tell you this. You can't let any man or person for that matter, steal your joy and get you off track. Whatever evil lurks in the heart of that man is of no control of yours. And the attempts to get you back by striping you of material possessions is all that he has to stand on. He is a man of no integrity or heart. You have a purpose in this world and God only gives us as much as we can handle. You are a strong woman, Yana, and you must continue to stand strong. Fulfill the purpose that God has for you in life. Not to preach to you, but this episode in your life with Benji is only a test in how you chose to deal with it. Life is full of choices...it's up to you to make the right ones."

He came and sat down on the edge of the bed and I laid my head in his lap and cried some more while he rubbed my back. His presence comforted me in a way that was much more than being intimate and I felt very grateful at that moment in the midst of all that was going on.

I looked up at him and said "Life is so crazy. I can remember when Benji used to bring me so much happiness or at least I thought. He used to always keep me laughing and now..."

Deleon interjected me and said," Well baby girl, just know that in the game of love the same thing that makes you laugh can make you cry. When you love hard and get hurt, that pain can turn to the deepest hate and anger that you have ever felt."

I just looked him in the eyes and realized how true his words were and I laid my head back down on his lap, closed my eyes and tried to think of more pleasant thoughts other than the reality of my

present situation.

## CHAPTER TWELEVE

I woke up under my blankets, snuggled tightly in my bed as the bright light from the sun pierced my eyes through the thin spaces in the blinds. I looked around and tried to gather my thoughts of what happened prior to my awaking and I realized that I wasn't alone when I fell asleep. I sat up in the bed and tried to focus my eyes as I looked from side to side, but seeing nothing except my clothes folded neatly on the chair in the corner.

I tried to recount the events of last night as I glanced at the clock on my nightstand, which read, 10:03AM. As I was putting everything into perspective I suddenly remembered that my damn car was gone and Benji showed his ass at Aunt Tammy's house. I was hoping that it was just a nightmare, but it was real. Then I wanted to put my head back under the covers and try and go back to sleep to forget the reality that I was living in at the moment.

Just before I was about to lay my head back down, I looked at the other arm of the chair in the corner and saw Deleon's sweater laying over it. But I saw no signs of him. Just then, my nose senses kicked in and I smelled the aroma of Aunt Jemima coming from my kitchen. I began smiling from ear to ear and as I pulled back the blankets from on top of my legs and started to get out of the bed. My journey out of the bed was quickly interrupted by a heavenly voice saying, "Uh, uh, uh little lady. Put those beautiful legs back in that bed, lay back and relax as you check out the cooking skills of Chef De."

As I looked up I saw him entering into my bedroom carrying one of my wicker lap trays filled with from what I could see, something out of a movie. He said, "Good Morning Sunshine. How are you feeling?"

I was trying not to seem ungrateful by the way I was looking at him. But I wanted so badly to go to the bathroom and get the crust out my eyes, the drool off my mouth and to brush my teeth, before I opened up my mouth to answer him. Lord only knows what I was looking like. But him, he still looked so fine, even in the morning. So I just mumbled through my lips, "I'm good, thanks."

Little did he know he could have put himself on top of that tray with a side of butter and syrup, and that would have filled me up just fine. But I gathered my dirty thoughts to the back of my brain and he sat the tray on my lap.

There was an assortment of fruits; honeydew, strawberries, cantaloupe, grapes; a stack of light and fluffy pancakes with butter melting slowly on the top; a glass of what looked like freshly squeezed orange juice and some eggs, sunny side up. Oh, I almost forgot, a beautiful array of lilies lay on the side of the tray as well.  I felt like pretty woman or someone out of a romance novel.  This had never happened to me before, but I could get used to this

I looked at Deleon and once again mumbled out the side of my mouth, "Thank you so much for this, it looks great. Could you excuse me for a minute? I have to go to the bathroom. I'm afraid of what I may look like right now."

He smiled and said," Of course hon. But trust me, you look just as spectacular as you always do."

Now I know he is a super sweet man, but now he is just plain lying.  I know I look like a booger bear in the morning, but I took the compliment anyways.

Once I was finished cleaning out all my ducts, I returned to my glorious breakfast in bed.  By this time he was sitting on the other side of the bed with his own breakfast tray.  I sat down next to him and he placed my tray back on my lap and we enjoyed breakfast and talked about yesterday.

I asked him why he stayed and he told me that he wanted to be here when I woke up, so he could help me sort things out. He went to the store while I slept to get everything. He just felt that me being alone after all the events that took place last night wouldn't have been a good idea.

After breakfast, I took the trays back into the kitchen and he followed me in there. He leaned up against the counter as I put the dishes in the dishwasher and he said that he would understand if I didn't feel up to feeding the men today. I told him, "I wouldn't miss it for the world. That's probably what I need."

He said, "Good, I'm glad to hear that. Also, I wanted you to know that I want you to drive MY car until we can think of something to get you back into another vehicle."

I just looked at him and thought to myself of how in the hell we gonna work that out with our work schedules? What is he talking about? So I asked, "How are you going to be able to do that? That's crazy. We live across town from each other and your work schedule and..."

He interjected, "I have another car, Ms. Lady. Why do you question my offer? If I say that I want you to drive my car, naturally I have things already figured out. Okay sweetheart?"

I looked down at my feet; feeling a bit embarrassed and said, "Okay, you are right and thank you so much. But are you sure that's not going to put you out?"

Deleon replied, "Not even a little bit, I was blessed with the ability to have both vehicles and my truck is at my buddy's house. He borrowed it a while back, but he doesn't need it anymore, so it's not even being used.  So I will go get it and you can drive the car.  Cool with you Ms. Yana?"

I know I was blushing when I said, "Yeah, it's cool." He walked over to me, wrapped his ever-comforting arms around me and gave me a gentle, soft peck on my lips. I got dressed and then we left to go to his house so that he could get himself together for our day at Joshua House.

His house was gorgeous and immaculate; it looked like a model home, you know, like the ones no one actually lives in.  In these past couple of months, he always comes to meet me or to pick me up.  I had never been to his house before.

He had a newly built three bedroom ranch, 2-½ bath, 2-car garage home in the airport area.  I was impressed, but I also expected it.  There was beautiful black art hanging up in just the right places on his walls and everything color coordinated so well.

Like if he had an interior decorator or better yet, some woman to decorate for him.

After he gave me a tour of the house, he led me to the den, where he told me to make myself comfortable while he got dressed. I sat down on the sofa and looked through some magazines on his coffee table. He had Essence, Better Homes and GQ...very eclectic selection.

After about 25 minutes he emerged once again, dressed all sporty and looking ready to serve some food to the folks today. I must admit I was very excited to be joining him. It was going to be a totally new experience for me and for such a worthy cause.

Once we arrived at Joshua House and pulled up in the rear of the building, I got somewhat nervous. I really don't know why I was nervous to be helping people, but I was feeling a bit hesitant to get out of his car.  However, I pulled it together and we walked in through the back of the building.

When we were approaching the building I was amazed at just how many hungry people there are out there.  It was shocking.  The line was wrapped around the building.  The people didn't look as I thought they would either.  When I think of food banks and people coming to eat, I guess I had the perception of them all looking like bums and being dirty and raggedy.  But for the most part most of the men looked normal. Of course they were nothing flashy, but not the scum of the earth either.

Once into the kitchen area I looked over towards the grill where I saw Mr. Jackson making plates.  He was such a humble man or at least that's the impression that I got from him.  I was glad that he and my auntie were friends; I think they may be good for each other.

Deleon waved and introduced me to the other volunteers as we walked over to Mr. Jackson. As he heard Deleon's voice, he turned around with his plastic apron and plastic gloves on. He had a spoon dripping with sweet potato in his hand, and said "Hey young people! So glad you could make it Miss Pretty. We need all the help we can get around here. I think this is the biggest turn out we have had in years. They must have known you was going to be here Ms. Pretty."

I said, "It's good to see you Mr. Jackson and I am glad to help out." He gave me a big hug and then stepped back and hugged Deleon too.

De said, "You're putting it on kinda thick on those plates Pops. If you keep feeding folks like that they gonna be expecting this every day." We all laughed and then it was time to get to work.

Mr. Jackson handed both Deleon and me aprons and plastic gloves so we could get started. I think the anxiety that I was feeling was coming from the fact that this was a food service job. I always had a phobia of working with food.

Even as a teenager when all the other kids in high school were getting jobs at places like Mickey D's and Burger King, I set my standards a little higher and worked in fashion retail instead. I just felt too embarrassed to wear one of those little paper hats and say" May I take your order please?, with grease stains on my doo-doo brown and yellow collared shirt and burgundy pants or whatever the colors of those God awful uniforms were back then. My mother would always say that I thought I was too good to work in fast food and for the most part, I think I thought the same. I could have never let the cool kids from school see me working there; I would have lost so many cool points. Most of them either didn't work or worked mall jobs like me. But as I reflect on it now, a job is a job and as long as it's an honest living then there shouldn't be any shame in it. But on the real, I went for jobs that were paying more than minimum wage and Ronald McDonald wasn't kicking out the dollars. So call me uppity, but I'd rather be saying cash, check or charge than, would you like to supersize your order?

But today is a new day and I am serving people food. I had to think that this particular group of people could have been me and I could actually be on the other side of that table. These men were addicts and even though I hadn't gone to any meetings or been in any programs, I had to face the fact that I had a drug problem that I was battling just as much as these men were. I am just fortunate enough not to have hit rock bottom because of it and to have some good folks in my corner to help keep me encouraged. So I am wearing the apron and the gloves and I even put on a hair net; can you say Bertha the cafeteria lady or what!!  But I turned my fear of embarrassment into pride and served those men until the last man came through that line.

I was having a great time.  I was spending time with De and I had the chance to talk to some of the men and I listened to their stories. It felt really good to genuinely laugh and even cry from hearing about their triumphs and their struggles.  I felt that I could relate to several of these men and some of them inspired me to keep on with my own fight for sobriety.  I don't know how to put it into words but somehow I knew that it was God that put me there on this day. Whether I was supposed to gain or give from the experience, I think I succeeded at both. Today was a good day.

## CHAPTER THIRTEEN (Year 2007)

The holidays were now over, it was now the year 2007 and it was back to the set for me. Deleon and I have been just as close as ever, spending a lot of quality time together and really getting to learn about each other as people. I was driving his Infiniti and he was back in his truck. So the fact that my Beemer was gone didn't really faze me because I could still accomplish what I needed to do. Finally every last remnant of Benji was out of my life. The good thing was that he hadn't even called or tried to contact me lately, which was a relief. So I was trying to stay in a positive frame of mind and keep pressing forward. But as the saying goes, there is always a calm before the storm.

It was time to get back to work on the set for me and things were really going great with my project. I was just wrapping up from shooting my second amazing fight scene and we were running lines for the next scene of the movie. I really enjoy working with my cast mates. It's still hard to believe that in less than a month I am going to be appearing in an actual film that people can go and pick up in the video store. Yes, I said video store. It's a straight to dvd movie. But hey, I am getting a paycheck and a girl has gotta start somewhere, right?

De and I had really been spending a lot of time together lately over the past few months and I was really enjoying everything about this relationship. We would often go to church together, have dinners out or at my place, we would go check out movies or rent movies at my place and just spend quality time lounging around on my couch. He said work had picked up a lot, so he was often busy, but he still was making some time for me. I noticed he was losing a little weight too, probably because he didn't have as much time anymore to work out like he used to.

Is it me or are you seeing that although we spend a lot of time together, it's always at my place? I am just now realizing that and I guess I never thought of it as a big deal or anything. He would always just come by my place after he was done with his appointments or whatever. I probably don't even need to be concerned with why we never go to his place. Things are so great between us and I am most likely just being paranoid because y'all know I'm not used to peace. Yeah, I'm sure that's it. I'm just trippin' thinking about something so petty.

However, even though we do spend a lot of time together, we still have been keeping our private parts to ourselves; which is literally driving ME insane. But I am trying real hard to respect the Christian aspect in this relationship. De is very affectionate and we do cuddle and kiss and rub a little bit here and there. But whenever stuff gets too hot and heavy he goes home. He tells me it's because he respects me so much and wants to capture my mind and heart, not my body.  I say, yeah, yeah, yeah, that all sounds good but a girl needs to get some sex pretty soon or I am going to burst.

I try to keep my mind off of lusting after his body by reading the bible and hoping a word will jump off the pages. Hoping a word will tell me that this abstinence thing is crazy and wrong and that it's okay to jump his bones as long as we pray afterwards or something like that.  (I am probably going straight to hell with gasoline drawers on for that comment.) But for real, I am not as strong as he is with all this church stuff and quite honestly...I want some sex!  I also have never had a man this wonderful and I don't want to ruin it on account that I am a horny little flea.  So I will try and be patient and hope that De will lose his religion for just a moment and give me some.  But until then, I need to go to Priscilla's Adult Store and get some toys to keep me occupied. I don't think God will mind that. That's not fornication if I'm doing myself, is it?

As my thoughts were wandering off into a land of lust and passion, my phone rang. It was De.  He must have felt my hot, panting breath through the phone because he asked if I wanted to get some ice cream later. I probably did need to cool my hot ass off.  He said that he had to run home first and change clothes and then he would be by to pick me up.  As he said that I thought of another idea. I suggested that I meet him at his place and we could go to Cold Stone Creamery out near his house. That would make more sense.

He said, "Oh, well sweetheart, I don't mind coming to get you. You know that I enjoy picking my lady up. That's what a man is supposed to do for his woman."

I replied, "I understand that baby, but Cold Stone is closer to you. That would be more like back tracking if you come to get me and then go back out that way and whatnot. I can just meet up with you at your place. I can leave now. How far are you from your place?"

De said, "Well Yana, I'm basically at the house already. So it will be a quick run in and out and we can actually go to another spot I know of close to your house. You don't need to come all the way over here. I will be your way in just a few okay?"

I said, "Ok, whatever. But De, why don't we ever chill out over your place? We always come to my apartment. We don't ever spend any time at your house."

De stated," There is nothing exciting about my house. Your apartment is much more cozy and in a convenient location.  Babe, stop trying to do so much.  Just let me come to you and we will go from there.  Sit tight and be pretty, I will be there in a minute."

"Umm-huh, okay" I said, as I hung up the phone.

Something just wasn't sitting right with me on this issue.  I wasn't sure of exactly what it was but let's just say my woman's intuition was kicking in and telling me to pay attention.  I didn't want to jump to conclusions because Deleon had never really given me any reason to suspect that he was up to something.  But you had to notice just as I did, he was persistent in not wanting me to go to his house.  So what was up with that?  I may not find out today, but sooner or later if he is up to some funny shit, it would come to the light.

## CHAPTER FOURTEEN

Today is the big day. My first movie is being released to DVD and I am so excited about it. I couldn't even sleep last night, just tossed and turned about the anticipation of how many people will see it. People I know and just people in general watching me on their big screens, little screens, black and whites or whatever. I would just be thrilled if a little old lady from Patterson, NJ watched it, which would be an achievement for me. It was all about the accomplishment that I actually finished something like this and I felt so good about it. Hopefully it would get some good feedback and buzz about it.

The director has done a pretty good job at getting the word out and marketing the project in all the right places. He even mentioned that it was a possibility that we would be attending the Sundance Film Festival. He told me that he was so proud of how well I did for my first acting gig and that there should be many more opportunities for me.

So in light of the big day, my cousin Terrance and Sharon decided to host a movie debut party for me at their place tonight. Mama and Tiana were supposed to be coming up from Charlotte tonight too.

Me and mama still weren't on that great of speaking terms, but she did at least apologize for betraying me with Benji during Thanksgiving. So I forgave her, after all she is my mother. But there is no way to forget that she sold me out for my psychotic, powder head ex-fiancée. But I wasn't going to have my day spoiled by anything, if I could help it.

I was on my way over to Terrance's house and I called him on his cell when I was leaving out to see if he needed me to bring anything or pickup something from the store, but he didn't pick up. So

I decided to call the house and speak to Sharon, also no answer. I got in my car and began to head over to their place. I had Sharon place an order at my favorite bakery, Sebastian's Dessertery, for the cake for my party. The bakery was located near my area, so I told her that I would stop and pick it up on my way to their house. I called her cell to see what name she put the cake order in, but still no answer. I thought she must be trying to put Tera down for a nap or something and Terrance was probably out putting some food on the grill.

I also called De and he said he was working late but he would be there later. So, I headed off to get the cake. The cake was beautiful! I placed it in my car and headed off to my cousin's house.

Once I got in front of Terrance's house, I called him again and called the house phone too, but no one was picking up anywhere. I needed some help to get the things out of the car. I just figured they must be super busy, so I just grabbed the cake and headed up to the front door. I was about to ring the doorbell but I noticed the door wasn't even closed. I was able to just push it open with my foot. At that point I was starting to get a little anxious.

I walked into the living room and tried to listen for movement or noise, the baby crying, the dog barking out back or something, but I heard nothing. I called out "Terrance!" "Sharon!" "Where are you guys at?" No one responded. I kept walking slowly towards the kitchen and I set the cake down on the dining room table as I passed through. Once I arrived in the kitchen, I got an eerie, cold feeling over my body as I saw the door to the basement cracked open. I crept closer to the basement door and I could hear voices.

The voices I heard were familiar but peculiar sounding. I was nervous because why in the world were they in the basement? It's not like they had a finished basement with an entertainment system setup or a bar or anything. It was just a cold, cement basement and I KNOW my party wasn't going to be held down there.

I gathered my thoughts and tried to figure out what I was should do. I tried to listen to what the voices were saying, but they were kind of low and muffled. My hands got moist and I began to get really nervous as I put my hand on the doorknob to approach the basement stairs. I slowly crept down each step trying to get a gauge on who was speaking and what could be going on.

Once I was able to get down the stairs low enough, the loudest voice became crystal clear as to who it was. You guessed it... BENJI!!! I just stood there in shock as to what I was hearing and at this point, what I was seeing. He was ranting and raving about how it's everyone's fault that he is alone and that they are the reasons I left him.

He hadn't noticed me yet because his back was to me. He was pacing along the floor waving that 9mm in his hand. The most disturbing part was that he had my cousin Terrance and Sharon tied up to chairs with tape over their mouths. It was like some real crazy hostage shit out of a movie. Terrance and Sharon could see me and their eyes just widened as to say "HELP US!"

I didn't know what to do! Should I go down and try to talk to him? Should I go back upstairs and call 911? But before I could get my plan together he turned around and spotted me. So I was stuck now. He yelled at me to come down and face him. So I walked down slowly. I just looked at the sheer terror in Sharon's eyes as tears were streaming down her face. Terrance was trying to remain cool, but I know he was unsure of what Benji would do at this point too.

I held my hands in front of me as to say, I surrender! I said, "Hey Benji baby. What's going on? Why do you have my family tied up like this down here?"

He replied, "Because it's their fault that you left me! I don't have shit no more. The feds ran up in the crib and I can't even go back home, they lookin' for me. This shit is all your fault Yana! If you was still with me, I would have been more on point. Them dirty muthafuckas caught me slippin'! One of those dirty bitches I was fuckin' with must have set me up." In the back of my mind, I was thinking THAT'S WHAT YOU GET BASTARD! But I wouldn't dare to say that at this point.

I just looked in Benji's eyes and I could tell he was past high and maybe on more than just coke at this point. His nose had blood streaks coming from it and his eyes were so sunken in, dark and hollow. He couldn't have weighed more than 145lbs, if that. He had on some basketball shorts, with black dress socks and black dress shoes and a dirty white button up shirt. Looking a hot mess! I was trying to scramble in my mind what to say or what to do.

I said, "Okay baby. You are right; I'm so sorry. I should have never left you. But Terrance and Sharon don't have anything to do with this. Please honey let them go." In my mind I wanted to ask, but didn't want to draw any attention to where the baby was. So I was just hoping and praying that she was asleep in her room.

Benji started waving the gun towards Terrance and Sharon, hollering, "These two sorry ass niggas got everything to do with it Yana. Didn't THEY take you in? Didn't THEY help you out? It's THEY fault I'm in this fucked up mess, so THEY need to pay!" And then he hit Terrance in the forehead with the butt of the gun and blood began to trickle from his head.

I desperately pleaded as I got closer to Benji, "Baby no, it's not their fault. It's all me. I was not thinking straight. I should have been smarter and I regret every minute of it. Please just let them go, so we can just forget all about this and get our lives back together with each other."

He was looking me directly in my eyes, so I really thought that maybe he believed some of the things I was saying. I didn't care what I had to say, I just didn't want him to hurt anyone; especially my cousin who was my heart and my best friend. Sharon was now crying hysterically since Benji had struck Terrance in the head.

Benji just kept yelling at her "Shut your stupid ass up before I shoot him!" Benji was pacing the floor again, sniffing a lot and rubbing the barrel of the gun besides his temple. He was speaking irrational saying, "Maybe I should just shoot us all! None of y'all niggas deserve to be here no way! Y'all ain't got a pot to piss in anyways. Might as well be dead! Yana, you don't even laugh at my jokes no more. What, you don't think I'm funny?"

I said, "No, no, no... Benji, you are super funny! You are the funniest person I know. You know you could always make me laugh with the funny things you say. Like this situation. This is the funniest joke you have ever pulled. So why don't we let them go and you can make me laugh a whole lot more later."

At that moment he put his head down and started crying. I was still keeping my eye on the gun. I wanted to go and console him, but that gun was just wavering all over the place. He lifted his head up and said, "Well, I think you are a lying bitch! You always loved this nigga more than me. So laugh at this!" And he aimed the gun at Terrance and pulled the trigger. Then he looked at me and said, "I always loved you." And he turned the gun on himself and shot himself in the head.

It was like everything was in slow motion. I heard the two gunshots and I looked over at Terrance. He was slumped over in the chair with blood pouring from his head. Benji was lying on the cold concrete floor with blood spewing from his head. It was a nightmare!

I ran over to untie Terrance and placed him on the floor to try and see if he was breathing. Sharon was in her chair having a fit. So I jumped up to untie her and told her to go call 911. She was screaming hysterically and crying, but I told her to please go upstairs and call 911.

I just held my cousin in my arms lifeless and limp. I put my hand over the hole in his head but I couldn't stop the blood, it was spewing through the spaces in my fingers. I just held him and rocked back and forth and I was just telling him to hold on.

Please hold on T. All I could keep saying was that I was so sorry that I let this happen. I kept telling him that I knew he was going to be alright...he had to be alright!

I just looked up and called on Jesus to please help my cousin. Since Jesus can do it all, then I know he can save my cousin. That's what De had always said. Jesus can work miracles, He saves lives, just keep faith and He will bring you through. Well Jesus I need you to show up NOW!

What should have been one of the greatest days of my life, turned out to be the worst! The ambulance and police came and got reports and they took Benji and Terrance away. Sharon was holding onto the baby, still crying and hysterical. Aunt Tammy was numb and speechless. Mama and Tianna had arrived by then and they were running around asking 50 thousand questions. I was just sitting outside on the porch covered in my cousin's blood and I just had to get away from this place. I had called De to try and tell him what was going on, but he wasn't picking up. So I decided to take the drive and go out to his house.

Once I pulled up in Deleon's driveway, I saw his truck and I pulled up behind a well-known car around town. It was a pimped out Chrysler 300 that was two-toned lime green and gray that belonged to Ozzie, the local male stripper and occasional dope dealer. So obviously Ozzie was here, but why? What would he have been doing with De? And why wasn't De answering my calls? All of a sudden I got that weird feeling all over again; something just wasn't right.

So I decided not to ring the doorbell, but to do a survey of the perimeter first. I peeped through the front windows, then the side windows. It looked as though I just saw a whole lot of boxes stacked up all hodge-podge over the place. There were no more pictures on the walls or decorations up anywhere. There was trash on the floors and I didn't even see his furniture in there anymore. It was like he was moving out or something. The house looked in true disarray, nothing like that first time I was there. But I didn't see him or Ozzie anywhere. I then headed back to his bedroom window. The blinds weren't as open as the others but they were cracked enough for me to see in. What I saw; no one could have ever prepared me for in a million years.

Ozzie was naked lying face down on the bed smoking on something. Deleon was standing over him with some kind of clear stick in his mouth smoking out of it. De was also naked and pleasuring himself with one hand and smoking the stick with the other hand. My eyes were as big as the moon! I couldn't believe what I was seeing. I then saw De put the stick down on the dresser and Ozzie raised his ass in the air. De then slowly inserted himself inside Ozzie, as they gyrated, grunted and fumbled around like two animals. I was mortified!!

I just ran back to the car, devastated, blood-stained, disgusted, and traumatized. I drove as fast as I could away from there with no destination, numb, mindless and beyond hurt from all that had happened in the matter of a few hours. There was nothing else to be said. I saw it with my own eyes. Deleon WAS too good to be true...he was a Gay-Crack Head!

All I could think was that this is the man who treated me like a queen. He brought joy and happiness to my life out of the darkness from where I came. He made me laugh and kept me happy. He talked so highly about God and never wanted to touch me because of his relationship with God, but now I know better! He, who was such a gentle spirit and kind and polite to me...wanted a MAN all along! How could I be so stupid?

Then my mind started racing to the fact that Benji, a man whom I loved for half of my life. Who made me laugh and smile, well in the beginning, has come to bring my life so much grief and pain. I still can't believe he just took his life right in front of my face. He's gone! Then he took one of the most important people in my life away from me, just as quick as he took all my material possessions away. It was like it was nothing to him to pull that trigger. His life was hell and I am sure that's where he will be for eternity!

I had to look up and ask...where were you God in all of this mess? Why didn't you do something to save my cousin? Why didn't you send me a sign or speak to me in the small voice about De? What miracle could be worked out now? What's the point? Faith had to be for suckers because it hasn't worked for me! I tried to believe and do better for myself. I tried to have hope and do the right things. All in a blink of an eye, things went from sugar to shit! Now my life has turned to pure hell on earth and that was WITH God in it! So much for trying to do things that way!

Three people died that day...Benji, Terrance and ME!!